# Montana's Come Up

## Marvin Lamont Loper

Montana's Come Up
Copyright © 2019 by Marvin Lamont Loper

ISBN- 9781088748091
Library of Congress Control Number:

Publishing Editing and Cover Design by
King and Queen Publishing, LLC
www.kingandqueenpublishingllc.com
Connect with us on Facebook and Instagram
King and Queen Publishing, LLC
Connect with the Publishers or to order contact
Julius and Queen
kingandqueenpublishing@gmail.com
publish@kingandqueenpublishingllc.com

This is a work of fiction. Names, characters, places, and incidents are products of the author's imagination and are used factiously and are not to be construed as real. Any resemblance to actual events, locales, organizations, or persons, living or dead, is entirely coincidental.

*Ded1catiom*

I would like to dedicate this book to my parents, Otis and Fannie Mae Loper (RIP). Thank you for making us Lopers.

What's up family? Turners, Roberts, Sanders, Oates, Heards and Fishers. To my sons Jaron and Marquise, I want something. Both of you are my hearts. Carlton and Rickie, wow it's been a long time, but y'all got me turned up!

To my siblings, y'all sheltered me and made me who I am. Y'all know lil' brah gonna make it happen. Lynn (big sis) I remember you the big homie. Things will be better. Thank you for the lifeline.

To my special BM thanks for holding things down and never giving up on me. To all of my nieces and nephews and greats, unc loves y'all like y'all are mines and if I blow up y'all going with me. Moo-Moo, and Lil' Ant what's up we will be there soon.

To all those that walked through the struggle like me, y'all keep y'all heads up, it only gets better. We make it happen.

To the down the way homies that fell before their time, we still miss y'all. Bull (RIP) KKO Hilltop hustler. To those that's playing the game. You're not a running back if you can't hold the ball. Stop fumbling it's just not you. To y'all stay up.

MTG 2001-2017

# Chapter One

*Montana*

*Crack Crack Crack* … Was the sound of the rocks Lil' Shorty threw at the window.

"What the fuck! Yo who the fuck is that?" Montana said as he got from underneath his sheets and reached for his old skool .38 with the duct tape on the handle.

"It's Lil' Shorty Montana!"

"Man you bringing your ass over here at 7:30am in the morning, waking me up while I'm laying up with my bitch. I started to let some hot ones go at your ass nigga, what's up?"

"Man, Case Court jumping. I just sold all the crack I had and I got this $650 I want to spend with you."

"You lucky you're my nephew 'cause I told you not to come over here to my house. By the way, let me get that $150 you owe me from the last package I sold you."

"Aw come on unc, I'm trying to come up. Let me bubble dis paper! I got you for sure. I'm about to go kill 'em right now. Old man James and Candy Gurl out there waiting on me right now."

"You ain't tell them you was coming over here did you?"

"Naw you know I know better than that, besides I want to be the only one out there with dope."

"Look here man, I'm gonna give you a whole ounce to work but when I get up and about later, you better have my $500 and don't bring your ass back over here for nothing without calling me!"

"Alright I got you unc."

"Ow! What was that punch to the back for?

"Oh that's because you fucked my sleep up, and you know I'm not right until I smoke a blunt and get my nut off."

"You lucky you're my nephew or I wouldn't be fucking with your ass. You keep fucking with them blunt strawberries, that's why you haven't came up yet."

"Let me get a stick?" Montana asked.

"I'm not giving you nothing," Lil' Shorty answered.

"I'm about to go wake my berry up after I sell my shit!" Lil' Shorty said laughing.

"What's this?" Montana asked.

"Oh you know I only fuck with the best. That's loud! I got that shit from the Mak-Mak's over there in Longwood Apts."

LA was the housing complex across from the Outhwaite projects on E. 40th Street. LA was known for its griminess. It was nothing to see someone robbing someone, someone selling crack or even seeing someone watered up on PCP laying on the ground getting help from someone while getting robbed at the same time.

"I'm gonna need more of that," Montana said.

"Well you better get up and go get you some more 'cause I'm gone," Lil' Shorty said to Montana, "time is money and I'm damn sure wasting my time and weed fucking with you."

"I'll holla back later!" Lil' Shorty said.

"Alright one baby!"

Montana walked back to the bedroom and Carmen was up going back and forth through her stuff.

"Hey baby what's up?" Montana said to Carmen while going in for a hug and a kiss.

"Nothing," Carmen answered.

"I'm glad you got me up when you did. I forgot I had to open up the shop *Ladies First* this morning," she continued as she kissed him and gave him a little grind.

"What time are you leaving?" Montana asked.

"8:30am," Carmen answered.

"Well that mean I got about a half an hour to get some head and play in that pussy, huh?"

"Ugh you nasty! You gonna eat this cake before you brush your teeth?" Carmen asked while laughing.

"I sure am 'cause I'm about to put this icing all on your face," Montana responded laughing. They laid on the bed. Montana kissed and rubbed all on her titties and pussy while she kissed, moaned and grinded her pussy in his face. After trading spots a couple of times on the foreplay side, Montana turned her over and doggy styled her the rest of the time, until they came together.

"Now get up!" Carmen said.

"Alright, but what time are you going to close the shop today?" Montana asked Carmen.

"I want to say 6pm if we don't have a lot of customers left."

"Well text me and let me know what's up 'cause I'm gonna take you to Len Rocks with Mack and his girl Poochie," Montana said.

"Len Rocks!" Carmen said while turning her nose up.

"Why Len Rocks? Them bummy ass hoes, none of them got shit on me," Carmen said while shaking and smacking her round 160 lb. high yellow ass.

"Well they got to start somewhere. Everybody can't jump up and make 200 bands in two years like you did boo."

"I know that; I'm just saying why are we going?"

"Mack girl Poochie gonna make her debut and we're going to support her."

"What do she look like?" Carmen asked.

"She nice, caramel complexion about 5'6", 145 lbs., long black hair with blonde highlights. She looks Black and Mexican, but she definitely got that money making ass."

"Oh yeah!" Carmen said.

"Yeah, for sho," Montana responded.

"Well okay, I'll text you and let you know what it is tonight," she continued as she put on a tight pair of black *True Religion* jeans with a baby blue *True Religion* shirt.

"Babe let me hit that stick you got before I go," she asked.

"Damn! How did you hear about that!" Montana responded.

"I was gonna take that to the head."

"You already took something to the head," Carmen said smiling and rubbing her pussy.

"Here smoke half," Montana said throwing her the weed.

*Damn! What a way to start a day. A good fucking and a blunt to go on the side*, Carmen thought to herself while putting the blunt down in the ashtray as she started out the door.

Montana said, "give me a hug and kiss and I'll see you later."

# Chapter Two

*Lil' Shorty*

"There he go right there!" Candy Gurl said as Lil' Shorty came walking around the corner of the brick building on Case Court.

"Where at?" Old Man James said getting up off the car and looking where Candy Gurl pointed.

"Right there!" Candy Gurl said.

"Well it's about muthafucking time. He took 20 minutes to get back. He lucky everybody still waiting for his bean head ass!" Old Man James said.

"Lil' Shorty! Lil' Shorty!" Candy Gurl yelled while waving her hands toward them. Lil' Shorty heard Candy Gurl and walked to where they were standing alone with six other people who wanted to cop what he had.

"Why the fuck you yelling my muthafucking name this early in the am like you crazy bitch? What you think I can't see or something?" Lil' Shorty asked.

"Naw!" Candy Gurl responded moving back and forth with her arm and poppin' her lips. She was wearing some old dingy, blue, white and black *Nikes* and some brown tight shorts that showed her pussy. She had no panties on. She wore a black *Fubu* shirt, that was also dingy from her staying outside for the last four days turning tricks.

"So what's up?" Old Man James asked.

"I got thirty, Candy Gurl got twenty and everybody else want something too. Make sure you bolt me up 'cause I stopped all these licks from going to the Compound," Old Man James said.

"I got you," Lil' Shorty responded, "wait right here for a couple more minutes and I'll be right back," he continued.

"Is his shit good?" Peaches asked Candy Gurl.

"He keeps that A1 dope and he's known to work that shake bag for some head or pussy," Candy Gurl said.

"I hope so 'cause I only got $40 but I'm not trying to spend all of my money," Peaches said.

"Aye y'all line up and let me know what y'all want," Lil' Shorty said after coming out of the bottom floor apartment.

"Let me get something for $8," a man said.

Then another man said, "I got $12."

Lil' Shorty grabbed their money and let them split a $20 rock. Lil' Shorty served the rest of the group until it was Old Man James, Candy Gurl and a caramel complexion, bow legged chic that was standing there. Lil' Shorty bolted Old Man James up for his services and Old Man James walked off.

Candy Gurl said, "I got $20 and she got $40, but we want to work something out."

"What the fuck you talking about y'all want to work something out? Candy Gurl please! I got you for your money but you know I'm not fucking your dirty ass bitch!" Lil' Shorty said.

"Nigga! Dirty ass! Fuck You! You're not working with shit anyway! Serve me for my money so I can go blow my thang!" Candy Gurl said.

"Here's a twenty and a ten and don't be yelling my muthafucking name no more because if you do, I'm not fuckin' with you no more. I'm not trying to go to jail!" Lil' Shorty said.

"Fuck you nigga!" Candy girl said as she walked off.

"So can I get served?" The caramel complexion chic said.

"What are you trying to do because your money ain't no good with me," Lil' Shorty replied back.

"Well I got $40, but I'm down for whatever as long as I get what I want," she said smiling.

"Turn around and let me see what you're working with then," Lil' Shorty said. She turned around and her ass was fat and round just like he liked them.

Lil' Shorty said, "yeah boo, that's what's up. Yo what's your name?"

"Who? Mines? It's Poo … Peaches," she said.

"Peaches what's up though," Lil' Shorty said greeting her.

"I already said as long as I get what I want I'm cool with it," she said.

"Well since you got $40, I'll give you two twenties and we can freak out," Lil' Shorty said.

"That's what's up Lil' Pimp," she said.

They walked down Case Court until they stopped at a three floor building with Lil' Shorty leading the way. They went up to the first floor apartment. Lil' Shorty whistled and a brown skinned lady opened the door saying, "did you see him?"

"Yeah, I seen him and I got something for you and Moe, but I need a favor. I need to use y'all bedroom," Lil' Shorty said.

"You know you're always welcome to use our room," Sue said as Lil' Shorty pulled a bag of dope out of his draws, giving Sue and Moe a rock a piece. Then he turned and gave Peaches two rocks. Moe looked at Peaches as to say *she smoke*, then he looked down because Sue was on his ass for looking extra hard.

"Nigga! If you want her, you can go get her and get your shit and get the fuck out of my house!" Sue said as she swung her big fist and caught Moe in the side of his head.

"Damn! What you hit me for?" Moe asked as he looked up at the short, Black 310 lb. lady wearing some blue jeans, a 4x t-shirt and a scarf covering up the wig she had on up underneath.

"Cause I told you about disrespecting me up in my shit!" she said as she gave Moe a look that said say something else. Moe got up and rubbed the side of his head and thought to his self, *if I had my own house I would be gone*. Reading his thoughts Sue said, "you can get your little, boney three pair of pants having ass out of my shit, you got some nerve!" she said.

Lil' Shorty blurted out, "Ma, daddy ain't even did nothing!"

"You don't even live here no more to know what's going on over here. You better go ahead and do what you need to do before I be putting your ass right back outside!" she said.

"Ma, you a trip!" Lil' Shorty said.

"Naw I'm not no trip, I'm a vacation!" she said as she walked in the front room yelling at Moe to come on.

"Sue, you gonna treat me better than this!" Moe said following behind her.

"Come on Peaches!" Lil' Shorty said as he walked her in a barely lit room with clothes and shoes scattered all over the room.

"Let's get down here on the bed." Which consisted of two mattresses, Lil' Shorty suggested.

"Okay Shorty, but first let me go out front and hit a piece of this rock before we start. I get all the way freaky off this," she said.

"Aw girl come on! I hope you're not the type that get all paranoid after you take a hit of this shit!" Lil' Shorty said. She grabbed his dick and stroked it a few times then turned around and rubbed her ass up against it making Lil' Shorty instantly hard.

She smiled and said, "naw, I told you I get freaky for real."

Lil' Shorty smiled and said, "hurry up!" as she walked out the bedroom.

She heard Moe saying, "come on Sue it's on me!" Thinking about the punch Sue gave him earlier, Peaches smiled to herself. She entered the front room that was just as junky as the bedroom, if not worse. There were McDonald's bags, Pizza Hut boxes and all these different jars were scattered all over the floor.

Sue and Moe sat on a sofa that had sunk so far in, they looked like they were on floor pillows.

"Excuse me," Peaches said. Sue stopped smoking her pipe and turned around to her.

"Yeah!" she said while blowing a big cloud of smoke out of her mouth and nose.

"Can I use y'all pipe to smoke this? I'll give y'all one of my rocks," Peaches said.

"Yeah, you can use mine, since I ain't got nothing to smoke," Moe said as he and Peaches traded.

"We're still splitting that rock!" Sue said as she gave Moe a look as he handed Peaches his pipe.

"I know that!" Moe said.

"Can I split it or do you want to do it?" Moe asked.

"I got it!" Sue responded as Peaches put her rock in the pipe and lit it and took a big hit, letting the smoke come out of her nose and mouth.

*Damn! Candy Gurl wasn't lying about him having some A1 dope,* she said to herself. As she handed the pipe back to Moe she said, "here y'all go ahead and finish this." Moe's eyes lit up. He was happy as hell until Sue snatched it out of his hand.

"Sue that's mine!" Moe said.

"I got you when I finish this," Sue said as Peaches walked back to the bedroom, still hearing them arguing about the pipe.

When she opened the door Lil' Shorty was laying on the bed. He had counted his money and rocks up while he waited on Peaches. Peaches started coming out of her clothes. She took of her *Baby Phat* jacket, wife beater and bra and stood there with her tittie nipples hard as hell. Lil' Shorty grabbed her hands and pulled her down to the bed.

"Are you ready?" he asked as Peaches answered, "you better believe it Lil' Pimp!"

# Chapter Three

## *Carmen*

*Ladies First* the sign read as Carmen pulled out her keys and opened the door. It was the place to be if you wanted to get your hair done in the latest styles. They did quick weaves, wraps, perms, dyes and anything else a woman wanted done to their heads and it was right in the heart of the city on E. 55th Street off of Woodland Avenue between King Kennedy and Outhwaite projects. Some of the roughest projects in the country at one point in time.

Carmen stacked her paper up and was able to get in on the reconstruction of the hood. For those who liked her, it was love, for those who hated, they were just jealous because she came out in the fashion that she did.

There were wall-to-wall mirrors with fish tanks built in some of them and marble countertops with top of the line equipment. As well as some of the baddest women in the hair game were working there.

They had clientele from Miami, Atlanta, California and New York coming right to the hood down the way and that brought everybody down the way to the shop, especially the ballers, hustlers and players outside looking to knock somebody nice off.

"Carmen!" Tara shouted as she walked towards her.

"Girl! You had me waiting on you. I thought you said you was gonna come in early and leave late today?" Tara asked.

"Yeah I did say that, but you know I had to get my freak on before I got here and you might have to close up tonight," Carmen said.

"Why?" Tara asked.

"Cause I'm going to a strip club with Montana tonight," Carmen answered.

"What Carmen, you back getting that paper?" Tara asked.

"Hell naw girl! Montana want me to go with him and Mack to support Mack's new girlfriend's debut," Carmen answered.

"The way I need money I should go and shake my ass," Tara said while fake dancing making her booty bounce.

"Well if that's what you feel, that's what's up but not at Len Rocks," Carmen said.

"Why not?" Tara continued her questioning.

"You know Len Rocks weak, all those busted ass hoes in that broke dusty ass spot. I worked up there back in the day and I thought those broke ass hoes was stealing out my locker. Come to find out it was the fat broke ass manager bitch!" Carmen said.

"Straight up? Aw hell naw I'm not going up there. I'll been done kicked somebody's ass!" Tara said.

"Hey there! What's up y'all!" Tee-Tee blurted in as Kay-Kay, Gail, Woo, Jackie and Bay-Bay who was a transgender male all spoke up in unison.

"What's up!" Carmen and Tara said back.

"Are y'all ready to do the damn thang?" Carmen asked.

"And you know this!" Bay-Bay said for the crowd.

"Shit girl I got three people that wants me to do their micro braids today, so please don't bother me cause I'm gonna have a attitude for real," Woo said.

"Well you better have your shit in check 'cause I been up all night drinking and I had to call the police on my baby daddy 'cause he tried to fight me over some pictures that was in my phone, so I'm not on no shit either!" Kay-Kay said.

"Well now that we got all y'all problems out in the air, y'all can start working," Carmen said.

"Oh yeah y'all, I want to let y'all know, I'm trying to rent a party bus and go to the D (Detroit), next week. If any of y'all want to go let me know. There will be food, drinks, strippers, male and female. Y'all can bring one friend each for $50 per person," Kay-Kay said.

"Damn bitch! You said that like you was doing some free shit!" Tara responded.

"Well if you're broke you don't need to be going no way," Kay-Kay replied back.

"Then count me out. I'm broke as fuck," Tara said smiling.

*Ladies First* was known to go hard on the customers, but this day Friday, August 5th it seemed like everybody in the city needed their hair done. You had the regular down the way chics flossing their do's, mixed in with the out of state chics and Cleveland's flyest all in one spot.

There were hopes of no one starting any trouble until this lady named Cream from California walked past for the second or third time and said, "damn Gail! For that girl to be bald headed and broke you sure are taking your sweet time on her head!"

"Bitch! I know you ain't talking about my sister!" Erica blurted out.

"What she say?" Be-Be asked.

"That bitch gone say Gail taking her time on that bald headed broke chic head!" Erica said.

"Bitch I will beat your fake Lil' Kim looking ass!" Be-Be said.

"Bitch don't get it twisted. I'm not worried about you broke ass hoes!" Cream said.

"Aye y'all chill!" Carmen yelled.

"Ain't nobody go do shit up in here. Y'all going to respect my shop! Thank you!" Carmen said.

"Carmen I'm not going to disrespect your shop, but that bitch don't know me to say shit to or about me. I haven't said nothing to her, but when we get outside I'm gonna show that hoe what a bald headed bitch from the 'K' will do!" Be-Be said.

Trying to change the mood Jackie said, "aye y'all, did y'all hear that the 30<sup></sup> projects boys got into with the Longwood boys last night at the Marathon?"

"What for? What!" Kay-Kay said.

"Girl, you know all these projects be going at it back and forth every time it gets nice outside and it doesn't be about no money. They be fighting over the new pussy that moves in the hood. Them niggas be fucking each other's baby mommas and be grinning in each other's faces at the same time and the girls ain't no better. They be fucking whoever from each project, thinking she ain't gonna get caught and before you know it, she has a baby by a nigga from all different projects and the shit hits the fan with her other baby daddies. The next thing you know they fighting back and forth. It's like a cycle 'cause it's been happening since my mother was born on E. 40ᵗʰ," Kay-Kay said.

"Well I hope Dee ain't got nothing to do with none of that shit because he's walking in right now," Tara said.

"Hey y'all! Damn it's some fine mothers up in here," Dee said.

"I ain't got no kids," Tara said.

"Well we can have one," Dee said laughing.

"Boy you need to quit, you already got two baby mommas," Jackie said.

"You next, but I want shorty right here now," Dee said.

"Leave my customers alone," Carmen said.

"Oh hey baby! I'm not bothering her, am I?" Dee asked.

"Naw he cool," Rhonda from Atlanta said.

"What's up tho boo? What's your name?" Dee asked.

"I'm Rhonda. Can I get to know you? I'm from the ATL, but I'm going to be up here for the weekend, so if you can get to know me by then, that's what's up," Rhonda said. Dee got her number and walked out the shop.

"Damn bitch you easy!" Bay-Bay said.

"Don't hate congratulate. I came up here to get my hair done and get some Cleveland dick, so that's what I might be up to tonight," Rhonda said smiling and waving her hand in the air.

"You nasty!" Bay-Bay said making everyone laugh.

"Aye y'all what's up with this Marathon spot y'all was talking about?" Kim from Miami asked.

"Oh girl that's the gas station across the street," Bay-Bay answered.

"Gas station!" Kim said.

"Yeah that's the place to be after the clubs close at night," Tara said.

"Oh yeah!" Kim reacted.

"Yeah girl they got all the food you want to eat and that's where the ballers and players be at, but you got to be careful cause all the project boys be up there starting shit and trying to rob niggas, but that spot be jumping with niggas," Woo said.

"I'll be up there for sure after we come back from the strip club tonight," Tara said.

"Strip club! That's right up my alley, can I go? "Kim asked.

"Shit I don't care, but I'm rolling with Carmen and her people, so it's up to her," Tara said.

"Carmen can I go with y'all? I got my own car, I just don't know how to get there. One of y'all can ride with me, if y'all want to," Kim said.

"I don't care if you come, we're just four deep already, but since you got your own car you can roll for sho. We're going to see my man's dude girl's debut at Len Rocks," Carmen said.

"Len Rocks!" everybody said at the same time with disgust on their faces.

"Yeah that's where she's going to dance at," Carmen said.

"I laughed when they told me too. I don't know her and I never seen her, but Montana say she cool people, but I'm not hip to her," Carmen continued.

"Well I'm gonna go to the mall and Tower City downtown Cleveland to get something to wear. I'm going to get me some *Gucci* clothes and Victoria's Secret undies," Kim said.

"Okay," Carmen and Tara said as Kim walked out the shop.

"Damn Woo you almost finished with your third head," Carmen said.

"Yeah girl, I'm glad too because my fingers are numb and feeling like they're about to fall off. If I didn't get $200 a head I wouldn't be doing this shit for real, but a bitch got bills for real," Woo said as everybody in the shop busted out laughing.

"Well I'm about to get ready to close shop when y'all finish y'all last head," Carmen said pulling out her cellphone to text Montana.

*Montana Baby, I'm closing and about to go home to get ready I-C-U later Love Carmen – Send*

# Chapter Four

## *Montana*

*Ring Ring Ring … Montana Baby I'm closing and about to go home to get ready I-C-U later Love Carmen*, the text read.

"Mack that's Carmen texting me saying she going home to get ready," Montana said.

"Well before we shoot to your spot, let's go down to Longwood to get some of that Diezel from the 3-0 boys, they say that shit raw," Mack said.

"My nephew hit me with a stick of loud this morning and that shit was fire. Me and Carmen was high. We can get a twomp a piece and we should be good until we hit Len Rocks," Montana said.

"That's what's up!" Mack said pulling up in the Longwood Apartments parking lot.

"Montana what's good big baby?" one of the youngens selling that loud said.

"Ow you know me, I'm just trying to make it do what it do," Montana said.

"Oh I got you!" the youngen said.

"As a matter of fact let me spend these two stacks with you," Young said.

"I got to shoot uptown and I'll bring that back down for you. Give me about 30 minutes and I'll be back. Man don't have me go get this shit and you ain't ready," Montana said grabbing the money putting it in the armrest, "I'll be back," Montana added.

"Make sure you get me right big baby," the youngen said.

"I got you!" Montana said.

"Tiger!" said Mack, "this shit better be good, having me standing in this long ass line like you passing out free cheese or something."

"Wha' gwan?" said Tiger, "what a boy like you want?"

"For standing in that long as line I want a free sac Jamaican boy," Mack said.

"Me don't have nuttin' free to give a blood clot nigga, but since yah my nigga, me a hook yah up man. Wat yah wanta buy?" Jamaican boy said.

"Let me get a twomp," Mack said.

While sucking his teeth Tiger said, "here you go man, that's Ganja so be easy," he continued while laughing and walking off.

"What's good Mack?" someone spoke.

"What's good Lil' Doobie?" Mack said as he walked back to Montana's black on black Infinity Q45, that was sitting on chrome 22" Ashantis with midnight tinted windows.

"Damn nigga, this car ride and sound good as fuck," Mack said opening the door to the sound of *Yo Gotti Live from the Kitchen* mixtape.

"You want to pick up Carmen then Poochie?" asked Mack.

"Who is she?" Montana asked.

"Man this Lil' hoe raw. She had a nigga fuckin with that white girl all night last night. I wound up falling asleep in that lil' pussy this morning before she left," said Mack.

"Damn straight up. Where you knock her off at?" Montana asked smiling.

"I was at the Top of the Flats and she was in there on the dance floor getting loose, so you know I shot my shot and she fell in my lap. You know that good hair and pretty eyes have a hoe thinking long term," Mack said.

"I know that's right. You full of shit though," Montana said laughing, "you told her everything about me except that I'm cocky and rich," Montana continued laughing even harder.

"Man fuck you, don't forget who turned you on to Carmen!" Mack said.

"Once I started poppin corn DTW style the hoe chose me!" Mack said laughing.

"Roll something up," Montana told him.

"What you want to fuck with first?" Mack asked.

"Man I told you my nephew gave me a stick of that Mak-Mak shit and it was fire, go that ..."

*Ring Ring Ring* ... Hold up ... hello?" Montana said answering the phone.

*"Where you at?"* Carmen asked as Mack picked up his phone and began dialing numbers.

"I'm on my way home, are you ready?" Montana asked.

*"Yeah I'm dressed. Oh! I told Tara and my girl Kim from Miami that they can come too,"* Carmen said.

"That's cool but how are they gonna get there 'cause we're four deep?" Montana asked Carmen.

*"Kim driving, she rented a Benz while she up here, so they can follow us."* Carmen answered him.

"Alright I'll see you when I get there," Montana told Carmen as he hung up the phone.

"Hello? What's good shawty?" Mack asked.

*"Hey there big daddy,"* Poochie answered Mack.

"Are you ready because after we go get my nigga's girl we're coming to pick you up," Mack said.

Poochie responded, *"I'm almost ready. I'm still putting my makeup on and making sure all my booty shorts hug my ass the way their suppose to,"* Poochie said.

"That's what's up! Make sure you're looking good because you're representing for the both of us," Mack said to Poochie, "oh yeah we going to the Marathon after we leave the club," Mack continued.

*"That's cool. Call me when you get here,"* Poochie said.

"Alright, I'll call when I get in front of the house," Mack said ending the call.

"Yo, what cha girl say my nigga?" Montana asked.

"She ready to make it happen on the dance floor. She say the booty shorts and the thong sets she got gonna make niggas go wild," Mack answered.

"Carmen said two of her girls are coming with us," Montana said.

"Who she talking about?" Mack asked.

"She said Tara from the shop and some chic named Kim from Miami. She say Kim up here for the weekend to get her hair done and she driving a Benz rental," Montana said.

"What she look like?" Mack asked.

"I don't know I've never seen her either," Montana answered.

"But we will see her tonight!" Mack said laughing while they pulled up to the apartment.

---KQP---

There was a crowd of niggas shooting dice in the walkway. One of the guys said, "what's up Montana and Mack what they hitting for?"

"Oh I'm on a mission right now," Montana replied, "I'll catch up with y'all next time!"

"Aye, let me holla at you," Lil' Tone said.

"Yo what's up?" Montana asked.

"Let me get two and a quarter, I got $1750 for it," Lil' Tone said.

"That cool, wait right here I'll be right back," Montana said as he walked into the apartment.

"Hey boo!" Montana yelled as Carmen came out the back room wearing some tight as black Capri pants. Some *Gucci* strap up heels with a red *Gucci* belly t-shirt cut down the middle to show her cleavage and a *Gucci* purse to match everything else. She was looking good standing 5'8" and

160 lbs., and honey light brown skinned. Her lips were super glossy which had her looking super sexy. She walked to Montana and gave him a kiss. Montana kissed and hugged her back while rubbing her ass and titties.

"Damn y'all get a room!" Mack said play hating laughing it off.

"This our house!" Carmen said.

"Y'all got some weed too?" Carmen asked as Mack hit her with the sack to roll up.

Montana came back into the front room and handed him a bag saying, "take that outside to Lil' Tone for me." Mack went outside and called Lil' Tone and handed him the sack and went back inside the apartment to the smell of loud.

"Hey now, let me hit that Carmen." Mack said as Carmen handed him the blunt coughing out smoke.

"Damn that's fire!" Mack said laughing hitting the blunt.

"What's up with your girl?" Mack asked Carmen.

"Who Tara?" Carmen asked.

"Naw the one from Miami?" Mack said.

"Oh that's my people she cool. She'll be at the spot with your girl tonight," Carmen said smiling.

"I hope so," Mack replied.

"Montana you ready?" Mack yelled. Montana walked in grabbing the blunt from Mack wearing a new all-black *True Religion* outfit, the new black and red Air Jordan's, a pair of platinum earrings and a platinum chain that hung to his stomach.

He handed Mack another bag saying, "hold that," then he put the .45 caliber and four grand he made that day in his pocket.

"Y'all ready?" Montana asked.

Montana turned to Mack and said, "we'll drop that off on the way."

# Chapter Five

## *Lil' Shorty*

*Damn* Lil' Shorty thought as he was smoking a stick of that good. *I'm going to fuck with her every time I see her.* Thinking of the way Peaches sucked and fucked him crazy wild.

*Ring Ring Ring*... Lil' shorty snapped out of his thought and answered his phone.

"What it be like?" Lil' Shorty answered.

"Short where you at?" the voice on the phone asked.

"I'm at the house on Case Court what's up?" Lil Shorty replied.

"Man it's going out here. I'm about to come through and spend this 400 with you," Boo said.

"Alright, I'm about to get up now," Lil' Shorty said hanging up the phone.

*Damn it's 9:15 p.m. Man that hoe put it down on me last night* Lil' shorty thought laughing to himself. Lil' Shorty hit the blunt a few more times and ran some bathwater until he heard a knock on the door.

"Who is it?" Lil' Shorty asked through the door.

"It's Boo!" he responded, "what's up with it?" he said as Lil' Shorty opened the door.

"I see you smoking that good. Is you ready for me?" he asked handing him the $400 and getting $600 worth of rocks back.

"Aye I'm coming straight back alright? Let me get the rest of that blunt," Boo said. Lil' Shorty hit it two more times before giving it to Boo.

"Good looking out. I'll holler at you later," Boo said as he left out the door.

*Knock Knock Knock* ... "Damn who is it?" Lil' Shorty said before opening the door up.

"It's Black Dee," Black Dee responded, "what's up with it my nigga!" Black Dee continued as he walked into the apartment.

"What's up with you?" Lil' Shorty replied.

"I got 800 for you," Black Dee said as he pulled out his money.

"Man I ain't got nothing for that right now, but you can give me $500 for this last $800 in rocks," Lil' Shorty said.

"That's a bet. Man you got to bless me later Shorty," Black Dee responded.

"I got you my nigga, I'll holler at you after I re-up later," Lil' Shorty told him.

"Okay!" replied Black Dee as he left out the door.

*Damn* he thought of Peaches again. Lil' Shorty picked up the phone and called Montana who answered hello on the second ring.

"What's up unc?" said Lil' shorty.

"I'm chilling about to go out to Len Rocks," Montana replied.

"What's up with you nephew?" Montana asked.

"Man I need to see you before you go out unc. I've got this $1,500 for you," Lil' Shorty said.

"I'm gonna swing past there before we go out 'cause I got to come over there anyway," Montana said.

"I'll see you later," Lil' Shorty said.

Lil' Shorty took a shower and put on a *Polo* outfit with the matching *Timberlands*. He rolled another blunt and walked outside before he noticed he ain't have his hammer on him. Lil' Shorty went and grabbed his .40 caliber pistol and put it on his waist. He knew better than to be caught without it knowing it's been shaky on coppin' dope. He stood there and watched as niggas hit their licks and smoked blunts.

"Lil' shorty what's up?" one of the dudes asked.

"Nothing!" he said walking over by the playground where there were like 20 people outside. They were doing all kinds of shit like shooting dice, smoking PCP and waiting to rob somebody.

"Lil' Shorty what's good my nigga?" Turtle asked.

"T what's up?" Lil' Shorty responded.

"Man, you know 30th and KK got into it last night, so make sure when you go up to the Marathon you don't get in the middle of that shit!" T said.

"What are they into it about?" Lil' Shorty asked.

"The bitch ass police Folley then shot the lil' nigga Boo Man from 30th and they think it was Pooh from KK that did it, so you know how that go," Turtle said.

"Man I ain't on none of that shit, but you know I got this .40 on me, so it is what it is, but in the meantime I'm trying to get this paper," Lil' Shorty said.

"Aye Shorty is your people on?" Turtle asked.

"I think so, but he 'bout to go out," Lil' Shorty responded.

"Well when you get time call him and tell him I need four and a baby," Turtle said.

"Oh yeah!" Lil Shorty said.

"Yeah man I've been doing my thing over in the Compound," Turtle responded.

The Compound is another part of Outhwaite projects over on the other side of Case Court, near the rec center PORC, also known as Pal Outhwaite Recreation Center or Lonnie Burton Center. This is where everybody from E. 40th hang, but all the projects be up there. It's where most of the chics be and everybody know if girls are around then niggas definitely coming. This is how the beef starts and how the beef keeps going on. For the most part E. 40th fuck around together and niggas can come and go on each strip as long as it's respectable.

Lil' Shorty's phone rang, *"hello … where are you at?"* Montana asked.

"I'm standing right here by POC," Lil' Shorty answered.

"Go over in front of your building. I'll be pulling up soon as you get there," Montana said.

"Unc it's all kinds of paper down here. I shot $3500 down, but they still down here. What you want to do?" Lil' Shorty said walking back to his building.

"Hey there!" Candy Gurl said coming around the corner.

"Lil Shorty you straight?" Candy Gurl asked.

"I will be in a few minutes. Why what's up?" Lil' shorty asked.

"I got $45 but I'm trying to get put on. I don't got no time to be getting high!" Candy Girl said smiling to herself.

"Come back in five minutes. I'll be straight by then," Lil' Shorty told Candy Gurl as she bent the corner.

Lil' Shorty was standing there as Montana pulled up. He got out the car and handed Lil' Shorty a bag.

"What's this?" Lil Shorty said feeling the weight of what was inside.

"That's a quarter bird I need you to serve your boy for the $3500 give me $1500 and I'm looking for $2000 tomorrow. Nephew don't be on no bullshit, get this paper and we're going to eat together," Montana said giving his nephew dap.

"Oh unc, when this lil' hoe come back down here, I'm going to turn you on to her. She raw with the head game," Lil' Shorty said.

"What's her name?" Montana asked.

"Peaches," Lil' Shorty asked.

"Peaches?" Montana said repeating the name.

# Chapter Six

## *Montana*

It was 10:30 p.m. Montana had sold his younguen some shit after he hit his nephew with a quarter bird.

*Damn that's nice,* Montana thought to himself, *but I'm ready to take it to the next level.*

Montana continued to think to himself, *I hope nephew steps his game up 'cause I'm about to start smashing it on him, but I know he be fucking with all them trick hoes. I can't risk a loss like that and I'm not trying to get caught up with this nigga for fucking with all these berries. I'm going to have a talk with him about it when I pick that paper up.*

"Yo Mack where your little chic stay at?" Montana asked Mack.

"She stay on St. Clair, but she just got a spot in the new Longwood on the 35th side," Mack answered.

"Well call her and tell her we're on our way over there," Montana said.

Mack called, *"hello!"* Poochie answered, *"what's up baby?"*

"Hey there! Where you stay at, we on 35th right now?" Mack asked.

*"Well keep coming down and I'll be in the door ... is that y'all in the black car?"*

"Yeah," Mack said pulling up.

*"I'm right here and y'all can come in,"* Poochie said. Montana, Mack and Carmen got out the car and went inside Poochie's apartment. She had one of the new apartments that were just recently built. It was like being inside the heights. Her yard had green grass and a new fence that closed and locked. Her door had a screen and a doorbell. We walked in and she had wall-to-wall thick crush carpet with a black and gold leather living room set. There was a large fish tank with tropical fish and black and white rocks at the bottom of the tank. She had black and burgundy Venetian blinds

with a red, black and white kitchen set. For Poochie to be living in the projects, it was very decent.

Mack introduced Montana and Carmen to Poochie. Poochie said she had heard about Montana and Carmen during the little bit of time she stayed down the way and it was all good things. She said it was a pleasure to be in their presence, which made Carmen feel trusting about her, but Montana on the other hand took alert, but it was cool for the moment.

"Carmen what's up with your girl?" Montana asked Carmen.

"They should be calling," she replied.

"You mind if we smoke?" Montana asked Poochie.

"I don't smoke, but I don't mind if y'all do," she answered.

"Do any of y'all want something to drink?" Poochie asked pulling the bottom of the couch bar out.

Tara and Kim called Carmen's phone, *"Where are y'all at girl?"*

"We over Mack's girl house waiting on y'all," Carmen said.

"Tell them to meet us at Len Rocks on Miles Avenue," Montana said.

*"Meet us at Len Rocks on Miles,"* Carmen said. After everybody was ready Poochie locked the house up and they all went and jumped in the Q45. Montana cut the music on and *Yo Gotti* started bumping out of the speakers.

*Damn I'm feeling myself,* Montana thought to himself.

"Mack what's up with y'all?" Montana asked.

"Shit we back here talking about this paper my baby about to get," Mack answered.

Carmen laughed and said, "you should've took her to Pinky's or the Bada Bing where them white boys paying off them credit cards. I'll tell you about it another time," Carmen said winking her eye at Poochie.

"That's what's up," Poochie replied back.

"Shit it do what it do everywhere," Mack said, "as long as she got this money maker, we're gonna always get this money," Mack continued squeezing Poochie's ass laughing.

"Montana do you want to get another sack to smoke while we're right here? Holla at youngen," Mack said remembering the package he had on him for him.

"I'll tell him to give us another twomp 'cause that other shit gone in the air," Montana said while pulling up in the Longwood parking lot.

"Young!" Montana called.

"Damn big baby you're right on time 'cause I got all kinds of licks waiting on me."

"Get that from Mack and let me get another twomp sack of that fire," Montana said.

"I'm going to make you a tab if you keep smoking all of my bud up," Young said laughing giving him the bud.

"It's all good, get back at me when you're ready," Montana said pulling out the parking lot heading up Woodland Avenue to Kinsman Avenue. As he slid across E. 131st and Miles Road, a red Mustang blew his horn at Montana and he stopped by his car.

Montana rolled down his window and said, "what's up Tito?"

"Shit man, I been trying to get at you. I lost my phone with your number in it. I got that paper for you," Tito said.

"Well I'm headed up to Len Rocks right now," Montana said.

"I'm going to go home and get that and swing up there," Tito said. Montana pulled off up Miles Road passing the funky fresh spot Joe D's Bar until he got to Len Rocks parking lot. There was a nice number of cars, but it was still early. Cars were still coming in and some of the dancers were getting off of work. Montana seen his dude Bango drop his hoe off. He knew T-Money from several strip clubs. She a woman that goes hard for that paper and she's nice looking at 5' 10" and 165 lbs. She was caramel complexioned and she wore a taper fade cut with waves spinning. She had her eyebrow, tongue, pussy and stomach pierced. Montana knew that from the time she was working at Magic City. Montana and Mack gave her $200 for a night on the town. Montana thought smiling to himself.

Poochie got out the car and walked in the club. Montana, Carmen and Mack sat in the car while they waited on Tara and Kim to get there. Tara knocked on the window.

"Damn girl! I almost shot your ass sneaking up on my shit like that!" Montana said.

"I'm not trying to get shot Boo-Boo!" Kim said.

"Y'all get in and chill for a minute before we go in. I'm waiting for somebody," Montana said.

"That's what's up!" Tara said squeezing in the back seat with Mack and Kim.

"I'm glad y'all got some weed 'cause I haven't smoked nothing since I've been up here," Kim said.

"Hey girl!" Carmen said giving both of them hugs.

"Y'all looking good, I want a hug too!" Mack said.

"That's Tara and that's Kim, she's from Miami," Carmen said.

"And you know this!" Kim said while reaching for the blunt.

"Girl I'm about to show these muthafuckas how we make it rain in Miami," Kim said getting her money together and ready.

"Make sure you hit my girl off," Mack said looking at the stack of singles Kim had in her hands.

"If she nice she's going to get some for sure," Kim said laughing blowing out blunt smoke.

"Aye y'all get ready, we're about to go in. There go my man's right there," Montana said. Everybody got out the car. Montana hit the alarm and walked over to his dude's car and grabbed the bag from him.

"That's $13,000 right there. I'm going to call you in the morning to spend my money with you," Tito said.

"Here's my number, get with me ASAP!" Montana said walking in the front door with the bag in his hand.

# Chapter Seven

## *Be-Be and Carmen*

"I can't wait to that bitch come outside!" Be-Be said to Erica.

"I can't believe this hoe had the nerve to come up in my stomping grounds and talk shit to and about me! I'm about to spray this bitch with this mace and beat the fuck out of her Erica watch!" Be-Be said.

"This bitch got me fucked up! It's gun play from the Killa K!" Be-Be said and they both busted out laughing.

"I started to flip out on Carmen, she letting these bogus ass bitches fly in from all these different cities and she's not letting these hoes know who's running this shit!" Be-Be said.

"Down the way!" Erica said.

"That's her right there!" they said as they got out the car and walked back towards the shop.

Cream stepped outside. She had on a brown wraparound skirt with a white button-up blouse that showed a lot of the titties she bought. She had a *Louis Vuitton* purse and *Louis Vuitton* sandals on. She had half of her hair braided in the front and it went into a curl in the back. Her hair was honey blonde with black highlights, which matched her complexion. She was tall for a woman, but her 170 lbs. looked damn good on her 6-foot frame. She had on Chanel glasses that covered her hazel brown eyes and half of her face. Her nails had a French manicure along with her feet. She had on a gold tennis bracelet, a gold Rolex watch, a big gold and diamond ring and a gold chain that spelled Cream.

"What's up baby girl?" a guy from the E. 40th projects named Cody said.

"Not much," Cream responded.

"You sure do look good and smell good. Where you from?" Cody asked. Before she could answer Be-Be ran down with Erica close behind her.

"What the fuck!" Cody said as the mace sprayed the air just missing Cream. Cream was quick on the draw. She stepped back and reached in her purse pulling out a chrome .380 semi-automatic pistol and pointed it at Be-Be.

"No cream!" was all you could hear from Carmen as she was coming out the shop.

Cody grabbed Cream and said, "ma you're too fine to go out like that!" Cream tried to pull away saying, "she got me fucked up!" coughing a little, but Cody was persistent with his strength and his game saying, "come on baby it ain't worth it!" Carmen came and helped him calm Cream down, while walking her back into the shop.

"That bitch got a gun!" Erica said as she pulled Be-Be's arm.

"That shit crazy!" Be-Be said as she replayed what had just happened.

"I tried to mace that bitch up. She lucky Cody was standing right there or she wouldn't have got the chance to get that gun. I'll still be beating that bitch ass!" Be-Be said laughing.

"Girl you are crazy!" Carmen said handing Cream a towel.

"Shit that bitch was trying to mace me!" Cream said grabbing the towel and wiping her face off.

"I was about to shoot the shit out that dumb bitch if dude didn't grab me!" Cream said angrily.

*Cough Cough Cough* … came from Cody as he said, "thanks for the love," between coughs.

"See Carmen you say I'm a bad guy and I do a good deed for your shop and get sprayed with mace, get called dude and didn't even get girly name or number, but I'm the bad guy!" he said making everybody laugh.

"That she crazy for real!" Cody said.

"I'm sorry baby I'm just salty that these hoes played crazy on me. I don't know what to do!" Cream responded to Cody.

"Well you can start by telling me your name and number. Then you can give me a hug and help me get this mace off my face," he said with everyone in the salon laughing.

Cream put her finger on his lips to shut him up then kissed him and said, "thanks."

# Chapter Eight

### Lil' Shorty

*Damn,* Lil' shorty thought to himself. *Unc fucking with me now. I wonder what made him hit me with the quarter bird. I ain't tripping because I'm going to handle it. He must have got a lot of this shit or he must got a new connect. Whatever it is I'm trying to be a part of it. I'm about to start stacking my paper now. Fuck all that bullshit.*

Lil' Shorty went into his apartment and broke the package out. *Damn this nine whole ounces,* Lil' Shorty thought. *I'm about to go weight.* Then he changed his mind and said to himself, *I'm a brick nigga. I'm about to brick rock these niggas to death.*

Lil' Shorty broke the whole quarter down except two ounces, cutting $2,000 per ounce. He was for sure to come up. He thought about all the shit he wanted to do and the shit he had to do. With that in mind. Lil' Shorty was on the come up. *Smile It's your boy Lil' Shorty!*

---KQP---

"Lil' Shorty what's good?" Old Man James said.

"I need you to run some notes for me alright. Go call Candy Gurl for me!" Lil' Shorty said.

"Okay Shorty. It's young dudes looking for dope too," Old Man James said.

"Well I got brick rocks, no weight!" Lil' shorty said, "tell everybody."

Candy Gurl came running around the corner. She had her money already in her hand.

"Lil' Shorty what you got for $40?" Candy Gurl asked him. He pulled out one rock and gave it to her. She took it and said, "give me another piece for waiting."

"I'll look out for you later," Lil' Shorty said.

"Alright remember that later," she responded hitting the corner with the brick in her hand just as fast as she came around it.

Old Man James came back with about ten customers. They were all saying let me get something for this and let me get something for that. Lil' Shorty served them all. Then he served Boo and Black Dee again, but this time he told them that he had it all day long and it wasn't going to stop. They both left happy and ready to serve their strips.

"I'm going to be straight back at you?" Black Dee said walking away.

"Shorty let me holla at you," Boo said.

"What's up?" Shorty replied.

"Front me some work my nigga. I'm trying to come up," Boo said.

"What you make off that last shit I gave you?" Shorty asked.

"I got $600!" Boo answered.

"Okay look here. I'm gonna give you an ounce. I want $600 now and tomorrow or the next day I want the rest. This right here is your chance to come up with me. You know where I came from," Lil' shorty said to Boo.

Lil' Shorty was adopted by Sue and Moe when he was 12 years old. He was living in a foster home for killing his mother while playing with a loaded gun. His father went to jail on a murder charge and was given life two months before he was born. Before his mother died she showed him all the love she could until she got hooked on crack. All the things he was used to getting was no more and it went to her crack habit. That's when Lil' Shorty went to doing what he knew to do. It started out as stealing a little money off tables and piggy banks.

His foster parent's kids had, but as time went on he started stealing out his foster parent's purses. One time when he was eight years old, his foster mother picked him up from school. They were home by them-selves. She laid down and her purse was slightly opened. Lil' Shorty could see the money. He knew if she caught him he would be in trouble. She would check his pockets and shoes when he went in her purse.

This time when he went in her purse, he stuffed the money in his underwear, but he didn't know she was watching him through a crack in the door. She called him and he instantly got nervous.

He tucked the money and said, "huh?"

"Go in my room and grab a towel for me," she told him. As he walked in the room she came out the bathroom with nothing on but her panties.

She walked up over him and asked him, "did you go in my purse?" Lil' Shorty shook his head no. She told him to empty his pockets and take off his shoes. Lil' Shorty did that.

She said, "take off your clothes." Scared, Lil' Shorty slowly started taking his clothes off, until he got down to his draws, where he stopped until she said, "take them off."

He grabbed at his draws and three $20 bills fell to the floor. With all his clothes off and the money on the floor, Shorty was caught red-handed and he broke down in tears.

She said, "muthafucka you stealing money from me!"

She grabbed his arm and shook him saying, "I got something for that!" As he cried in hurt and fear, she took her panties off while he was standing there crying and naked. Her dark brown complexion stood, 5' 7" and she had big titties that hung.

She kept saying, "you stole my money!" She pulled his face into her hairy muff.

She screamed, "lick it since you stole my money, lick it lick it!" She grinded and moaned in his face until she came all over him.

"Now pick that money up and go put your damn clothes back on!"

She yelled, "and wash your face!"

Over the next few months she was calling Lil' Shorty in her room. She started making him get on top of her and hump her and things were going okay, until she caught him and her 12-year-old daughter getting it on. Lil' Shorty was eating the shit out of her daughter's coochie and like daughter, like mama, she was laying there loving it.

"Aw hell naw!" she yelled, "I'm taking you back to foster care!" And from that time on Lil' Shorty had a thing for sex.

He started putting it down and in foster care is where he met Boo, who was Lil' Shorty's age and they bonded. They were from the bricks and both of them wanted more out of life.

"On the bricks I got you and your money Lil' Shorty," Boo said, "outlaws forever."

# Chapter Nine

## *Montana*

When they walked in the club it was slightly dark. The dancers were walking around with their asses out. Kim went to the bar and ordered three bottles of Moet and got two hundred in one dollar bills. Montana and Mack both got one hundred singles a piece too. Montana gave Carmen half of his bills. They sat down at the back table. Dancers came past and they all put a few dollars on them. At first Montana didn't want any lap dance until a girl named Booty walked by and caught his eye. He was about to let her pass until Carmen stopped her and said, "aye Boo-Boo come and dance for my nigga," holding some dollar bills out. She came over to their table. She was a light caramel chic with big hazel green eyes. Her hair was cut low on one side with the word Booty cut in her head. The other side was long and black with red tint. She had some white booty shorts on with a white bikini top. Her legs were lightweight slim, but her ass was nice and round. It wasn't very big, but it was nice nonetheless.

She was 5' 6" and with heels she was 5' 8" and 155 lbs. The DJ was playing, *Round of Applause Let Me See That Ass Clap by Waka*. She started shaking her ass crazy. She was bouncing one cheek then both cheeks. She was going hard. They all made it rain on her and that made her go harder. She got on her knees and bounced her ass, until the song stopped.

"Damn, girly putting it down!" Montana said as he popped a bottle.

Kim shouted, "hell yeah I am strictly dickly, but I'll let her licky lick me any day!"

"Girl you nasty, she went hard but not that damn hard!" Tara said laughing and filling up her cup. Mack was sweating. He took off his hat to wipe his head.

"She was nice!" he said as he thought about fucking her.

The DJ kept playing booty dancing songs until he said, "I'd like to welcome Poochie to the stage!" She came out to R Kelly's *TP3 Feeling On Ya Booty*. She had on a red and white thong and a red top. She had her hair black, long, curly and wet looking with glitter on her body.

"Damn Mack your girl got it going on, don't she Boo?" Montana asked Carmen.

"Yeah she looks nice, if she get to the right club she can make some real money." Carmen answered. Poochie sat on the stage and opened her legs wide. You could see the crease of her pussy through her thong as she rolled and waved her body forward. Kim and a couple of other people made it rain on her with dollar bills.

One dude yelled out, "I got two hundred for some of that pussy!" She got on all fours and spread her ass open and they made it rain again. She stood in a doggy style position making her ass cheeks clap and bounce up and down before spreading them causing the onlookers to throw more money and cheer for her more.

She was about to get off the stage, but everybody was still throwing money and popping bottles yelling, "one more dance!"

The DJ started playing, *Juvenile's Back That Ass Up* and Poochie began to go ham. She really started to back that ass up. The other dancers saw how she was racking in the paper and made their way over to try and steal some of her shine. Kim and Carmen noticed it and told them hoes to kick rocks and to find another spot to dance before they got their asses beat. They kept it moving to back that ass up.

After that song, Poochie went and joined everyone and they showed her love and gave her hugs as if they all knew one another forever.

Kim popped another bottle and told Poochie that muthafuckas in Miami would love her.

Mack picked Poochie up saying, "baby we're going to get this money."

"For sho!" Poochie said as she thought of somebody else to herself.

Montana said, "aye y'all it's almost 2:00am. I'm ready to leave here and go smoke me a blunt and slide down to the Marathon to get something to eat."

"That's what's up," Mack said as he began to count the thick wad of dollar bills Poochie handed him to count. She went to get dressed. Poochie came out of the dressing room wearing a powder blue Baby Phat jogging suit.

Montana said, "Mack your girl did her thang my nigga. Y'all should build something together, if you keep her."

"She's mines fo sho," Mack said still counting the $680 in bills Poochie made.

Tara and Kim stood to the side talking to one of the dancers named Co-Co.

"What's up baby girl?" Kim asked playfully.

"Nothing now!" Co-Co responded hoping Kim wanted to kick it with her afterwards.

"Naw baby, I just spoke," Kim said as she thought about going home with Co-co.

It was tempting as Co-Co licked her lips and said, "I'll have my way with you pretty."

"I know that's what's up, but I'm cool," Kim said as she thought about Poochie and the chance to get at her. It would be only her second time but that's what she wanted and if it was money that it took then money it would be.

Montana walked up and told them to follow him down to the Marathon. Kim said okay but she told Montana she was a little bit tipsy in a slurred stutter.

"Well look here, Mack drive with Kim and Poochie and I'll take Tara with me and Carmen," Montana instructed.

"Where are we going?" Mack asked.

"Down to the Marathon," Montana answered. Kim got in the back seat of the Benz and Mack drove off.

Kim and Poochie was flirting back and forth with each other when Mack asked, "why don't one of y'all fire up a blunt for me."

"I got you, because I need a stick too!" Kim said.

They pulled up in the Marathon parking lot and there were people and cars everywhere. Three men were standing on the side of the building by the trash dumpster smoking cigarettes dipped in water (PCP).

One of them were trying to talk to a lady passing by saying, "heyyy babyy what up?" He stuttered two times before forgetting her and grabbing the squally again and puffing it. Carmen and Tara walked into the Marathon and ordered some food. Montana walked over to where Mack, Poochie and Kim were standing by the carwash on the side of the Marathon. The carwash had music blasting out of it. There was a white Corvette being washed by six women all dressed in bikini tops and daisy duke shorts.

"Damn this shit is off the chain!" Kim said looking at them. She pointed towards the chics washing the cars.

"Yeah it goes down here!" Montana said as niggas walked up speaking to them. There were people coming from all the clubs in the city of Cleveland. Most of them were from down the way. It was down the way, but you had niggas from Hough, Cedar, St. Clair, Kinsman, Harvard, Shaker Hts., and East Cleveland, however it was the women from there too. Niggas were hollering at the hoes and the hoes were trying to get at that paper. So anything was bound to happen. They walked into the gas station.

"Assam akum," the Arab said as they walked to the counter.

"What's good," Montana said as he gave him dap and exchanged handshakes.

Mack asked, "Talib what's the price on tha vet you got them chics washing?"

"You got the money you can get it right now," Talib answered.

Talib was an Arab that grew up in Cleveland. He's been in the country since he was 11 years old. He started working in the hood at 14 years old and from there, he did everything people did in the hood. He smoked good, sold good cocaine and he loved Black women. It was nothing to see Talib in a car or on a bike with a Black chic on the back riding shotgun.

Mack ordered Poochie and Kim something to eat. Once they got their orders they heard, *Pop Pop Pop Pop Pop Pop.* Instantly everybody ducked down and ran for cover. There were two different clicks of projects outside fighting. KK and 30th were going at it in the street. Longwood and the Compound was on the side of the carwash getting it on as well. Montana punched a few niggas as he got in his car and grabbed his gun.

"Mack is y'all cool?" Montana asked.

"Yeah we cool. We about to go to the house. Y'all want to roll? Kim's gonna stay with us," Mack said laughing and smiling, "I got 30 bands I want to spend tomorrow, so be ready."

"Oh I got you fo sho, but I got to re-up," Montana responded.

Kim thought to herself as she stuffed her face with the corn beef sandwich, *it's going down tonight.*

# Chapter Ten

### *Mack, Poochie and Kim*

Montana and Carmen took Tara home. She was tipsy, but she was feeling herself. *I had a good time,* she thought to herself. *Like I'm bad my muthafucking self! I should have got my ass on that stage and shook my ass for that paper.* Tara continued to think laughing to herself. *I'm gonna holler at Carmen to see what spot I can come out at.*

Montana and Carmen got home.

"Damn baby, I'm feeling myself and I love you," he said, "I'm not gonna do this forever. I want more out of life and I want to give you more. I've been in the streets all my life and I want one more shot at this paper and it's retirement from there."

"Life is too short, but I'm with you to the end," Carmen replied to him, "I can tell my girl Kim to turn you on to her people," Carmen continued.

"Your girl Kim people got that weight (dope)?" Montana asked.

"Yeah they do. They family should be a team in the NBA because they balling for real."

"Why you ain't been tell me that?"

"Cause I don't be all in your street business, but I'll ask her when I talk to her."

Montana picked up his phone and called Mack's phone.

*"Hello, What's up?"* Mack answered.

"Man we looking for a hook and you got the bait right there," Montana said.

*"Strait up?"* Mack responded.

"Yeah man," Montana said to Mack.

*"Well let me get back at you before I miss this party."*

"What?"

"Montana I'll call you back," Mack said hanging up the phone.

Mack, Poochie and Kim were sitting in the living room. Mack and Kim were smoking a blunt. Mack asked Kim if she knew somebody in Miami he could spend some paper with.

Kim asked back, "what type of paper you talking about?"

"Like 100 stacks," he answered.

"For real!" Kim reacted.

"Yeah baby, I'm for real. I'm trying to come up and find me a thorough connect where I can get some better prices and better quality. I'll spend more if shit go right," Mack said.

"I'm from Miami where shit go for real, but I'm gonna tell ya, muthafuckas I fuck with they don't play about this money shit, so think about what you want to do before you do it because it's Miami love, but it's blood in blood out," Kim said, "that's that and this is this."

"What's this?" Mack asked Kim rubbing her booty.

"I want to get down with y'all tonight," Kim said.

"Poochie what's up with this?" Mack asked.

"I told her to ask you, so it's your call," replied Poochie. Mack kissed Poochie as Kim came from the back and sandwiched her. Mack, Poochie and Kim all started kissing each other while easing each other's clothes off.

Kim unfastened her bra and let her titties fall out. Kim was hugging Mack and kissing Poochie. Poochie took off everything except her panties, while Mack stripped down naked. He grabbed the blunt out the ashtray and blazed it up and walked upstairs. It was like they followed the smoke trail, the way they were right behind it.

They went into the bathroom where Poochie took off her panties and got into the shower. Kim followed suit, while Mack sat on the toilet and puffed on the blunt a few more times. As he stood up they were kissing under the water. He reached and grabbed their asses and then he rubbed their pussy from the back. Slowly putting his finger in their pussies going in and out. They both kissed, rubbed and reached for Mack's dick. They stroked him until he was ready. He grabbed Poochie and went to turn her around to fuck her, but Kim said, "Mack get me."

Mack turned her around and bent her over. He grabbed her hips and slowly entered her wet pussy. Her ass was soft and jiggly as he gripped it. She pulled Poochie towards her and went down and began to eat her pussy.

Mack pounded Kim's pussy from the back and rubbed Poochie's titties. Poochie moaned, Mack moaned and Kim grunted.

Kim lifted her head and said, "damn baby you misfired with that last pump!" Mack and Poochie busted out laughing.

"Girl!" Poochie said, "Mack always accidentally slipping a bitch in the ass!"

"Y'all sitting there laughing! I'm not on that!" Kim said as she walked to Poochie's bedroom and laid on the bed with her legs wide opened. Mack walked into the room.

"I was wondering when somebody was coming to get this pussy," Kim said.

"Well baby no need to worry, I'm about to take care of that for you," Mack said climbing down and eating her pussy. He licked all down her leg then up the other side, while sticking his finger in and out of her pussy. She moaned while he licked his fingers and rotated them back to her.

She was so wet. She started pumping his face. She grabbed his dick and started stroking him. While he was eating her out he flipped her over and they went 6-9 style. They were going at it so much they didn't even notice when Poochie looked in the room and saw them in the 6-9 position.

She turned and went downstairs, put on her clothes and walked outside with a stack of her one dollar bills. Mack was on top of Kim pumping away when he heard the vibration of his phone texting.

*Zzz Zzz Zzz ... Mack I went outside to get some air. We got money* Poochie texted.

"That was Poochie she said she went outside to get some air," Mack told Kim.

"She left?" Kim asked.

"She'll be back," Mack said thinking about finishing the nut he was almost at. He got back to doing his thang until they both climaxed.

Mack rolled over and said, "we got to talk some more."

# Chapter Eleven

## Lil' Shorty

Lil' Shorty was standing outside on Case Court. He had almost five stacks from selling the large rocks. Rock for rock, the word got around quick. It was about twenty minutes after Lil' Shorty got that pack and broke it down that everybody that smoked and hustled was on Case Court to cop some work from him.

Lil' Shorty was loving it. He served them and as fast as he did, people were coming back buying again and again.

*Damn, I'm coming up* Lil' Shorty thought to himself, *I'm gonna finish this bag then I'm going to go get me something to eat from the Marathon.*

Lil' Shorty was ready to go, but a lot more people came wanting crack. He stayed and sold another whole bag of rocks.

Man-Man, Moe, CB, Slick and Pimp was walking down Case Court. Lil' Shorty wondered what they were up to so he asked them.

"What's up y'all? What y'all up to?" Lil' Shorty asked them.

"Man we looking for that nigga Marvel!" Slick said.

"What for?" Lil Shorty asked, "he just left from over here."

"That bitch ass nigga just broke in Man-Man's car!" Slick said.

"I think he walked toward the Marathon, but I ain't sure," Lil' Shorty said, "Man if y'all need some dope I got the hook on whatever, so get at me on that side y'all," Lil' Shorty continued.

"Straight up?" Pimp asked.

"Yeah man I got whatever … look," Lil' Shorty said showing them the rocks.

"Damn what these go for?" CB asked.

"Twenty-five dollars apiece," Lil' Shorty said as he put the bag back in his draws.

"I'm gonna roll with y'all. Let me take these rocks in the house," Lil' Shorty said as he walked towards his building.

Lil' Shorty came back outside and they all started walking towards the Marathon. Lil' Shorty saw Old Man James and Candy Gurl as they walked down the street.

"Lil' Shorty you gone for tonight?" Old Man James asked.

"What the fuck I tell y'all MF's!" Lil' Shorty said.

"What I say wrong?" Old Man James asked.

"I told you and Candy Gurl both that I'm not trying to go to jail, so stop asking me shit when I'm with people. Pull me to the side!" Lil' Shorty said.

"My fault Shorty! I just wanted to tell you that the chic Peaches looking for you," Old Man James said.

"Straight up? Where she at?" Lil' Shorty asked.

"She up the street," Candy Gurl said, "you want us to tell her something?"

"Tell her I said I'll be back in a minute and to wait for me okay?" Lil' Shorty said.

"Alright Shorty," Old Man James said.

As they were headed in different directions Lil' Shorty looked back and said, "ain't that Detective Folley bitch ass?"

"Where?" Man-Man said as everybody else looked around for them. They pulled their car right up on them. Lil' Shorty asked everybody was they clean and before anybody could say anything Man-Man took off running, which meant run in the hood. Everybody ran up to the Marathon. When they got up there it was crowded, so they just blended in. Lil' Shorty was so glad because he fo sho fo sho had his hammer and some money on him.

They mingled through the crowd hoping to see Marvel. They looked over to see if he was on the side of the building smoking water with the other dudes, but it wasn't him. They started hollering at the KK niggas to see if they saw Marvel. Soon as Lil' Shorty asked that question and let them know he had some dope to sale for the low, the D30 boys came up like, "ain't that the KK niggas?" he heard one of them say, "it's 30$^{th}$ this way!"

Before you knew it, they were fighting and it was an all-out brawl, 15 against 15. It was a good match until somebody said police and half of the KK niggas took off running and left the other half fending for themselves.

Be-Be ran in the crowd spraying mace and waving the can in the air saying, "get off my baby daddy muthafucka! Y'all bummy ass 30$^{th}$ niggas always trying to jump somebody!"

When they got over the mace. Lil' Shorty looked over and Longwood and the Compound boys started fighting. They were all on people cars. People were getting hurt for just being there and close enough to get punched. They were all fighting each other.

As the fights continued on, they started robbing people that wasn't from the projects. You heard the sirens from the police, but by the time they got there it was about four dudes knocked out on the ground and six people were robbed. The police were arresting a few people for disorderly conduct.

---KQP---

Lil' Shorty and the crew went back into the gas station and ordered some food. It had been all day since Lil' Shorty ate. He got some donuts, juices and a huge extra-large corned beef sandwich.

"Damn you must haven't ate since your last package," Pimp said making everybody laugh.

"Naw nigga it ain't that. I'm just getting this paper now. Doing me. Y'all niggas want something?" Lil' Shorty asked.

"I don't want nothing but to catch up with Marvel for breaking in my car. That muthafucka know I don't be playing no games with niggas!" Man-Man said.

"Let's go back on Case Court and see if he came back through there," Pimp said.

"I'm about to go back and get my hustle on. I'm full now. All I need is a nice blunt and a shot of head and I'll be cool for the rest of the night," Lil' Shorty said.

"Aye Shorty how you say you selling that work?" CB asked.

"I got some bricks going twenty-five for twenty-five," Lil' Shorty answered.

"Aw man, Lil' Shorty I didn't serve you like that when I was on!" CB responded.

"I know, that's why you're not on no more!" Lil' Shorty said laughing.

"I'll make sure you're straight but I got to get rid of this pack right here first. Then I can do something for however much money you got," Lil' Shorty told CB.

"Alright Shorty," CB said, "make sure you bless me my nigga!"

"You know I'm gonna look out for you. My nigga you know I got down the way love!"

When Lil' Shorty got back on Case Court it was so dark that he couldn't even see the three people walking towards him.

"Lil' Shorty is that you man?" Old Man James asked.

"Yeah it's me what's up?"

"Man everybody been over here looking for you," Old Man James said.

"Well I'm right here now," Lil' Shorty said.

"Hey there Lil' Pimp!" Peaches said.

"What's up!" Lil' Shorty said giving her a hug.

"What you doing out this late?"

"I'm out here messing with Candy Gurl and Old Man James."

"Oh yeah!"

"Yeah I got $60 I want to spend with you."

"Well you know I usually say your money ain't no good with me, but I'm trying to come up with this paper, so everything I'm doing is to come up."

"I feel you!"

"Yeah baby besides that where have you been at?"

"I'll tell you about it later after I look out for Old Man James and Candy Gurl. I'll be back to let you know what's been going on with me."

Peaches, Old Man James and Candy Gurl walked across the courtyard into a dimly lit hallway that was littered with trash and smelled like piss from people urinating in the corners. As they walked up the stairs there was a young dude getting head from a strawberry. They acted like nobody even existed because they didn't miss a beat as they walked past. They kept rolling by when the young dude said, "come on baby I'm about to come!"

They walked past them to the top of the stairs landing. Candy Gurl pulled her stem pipe out of her sock and handed it to Peaches saying, "this yours." She pulled her other one out of her pocket. Peaches gave both of them a rock a piece and started smoking the last rock herself. She hit it a few times and said, "I'm cool, that's enough fo me."

"Aye!" she called to the lady downstairs that was arguing with the young dude about her pay.

"Yeah!" the lady said.

"Do you want a piece of this rock I got up here?" Peaches asked the lady.

"Yeah, but I don't have no money."

"Here you go it's on me," Peaches said as she walked out of the building back to where Lil' Shorty was at.

"Damn girl you smoked that shit that fast?" asked Shorty.

"Naw I gave that shit to them after I took a few hits!" Peaches said.

"So why do you smoke if you really don't smoke?"

"I like the high."

"So what you trying to get into?" Shorty asked.

"I don't care, it's up to you. I had a good time the last time we were together," Peaches answered.

"I did to."

"I thought about you all day," she told him.

"What did you think about?" Lil' Shorty asked her.

"How I felt good, when I was with you and how I could help you." Peaches answered him blushing.

"How can you help me?" Lil' Shorty asked.

"Well I started dancing today. I liked it and I made a lot of money," she said, "I know I can help you because I know people that's doing something that's up your lane."

"Oh yeah well I'm definitely gonna need you baby," Shorty said, "and what's this dancing thing you started?"

"Well I debuted today at Len Rocks," Peaches said.

"Is you good? I want to see you dance to see what you're working with," Shorty said looking at her as Peaches turned around and made her booty wiggle a little. That opened Shorty up. He grabbed it and rubbed it and asked Peaches if he could have some of her ass.

She liked Lil' Shorty. She told him that he could have anything he wanted from her. Shorty smiled at her and asked her what did she know about the game he was trying to succeed in. She told him she had a girl that liked her and all her people were from Miami. They had hooks on the drug side and this guy she knows was about to get hooked up with her friend's people and she could hook him up with them when he gets his money up. She told him she could help him stack his paper and she would start giving him what she made and when she finds out where there putting their money at she will set it up, so he can get it.

Shorty grabbed her and said, "it's a lot we got to get through. I know I got shit I want to do and there's things I need to do and if I ever get the chance, I'll make sure I take you with me, but before I'm able to do what I do you got to get yourself together. I can't have you getting high off crack!"

She reached for his pants and pulled him closer to her and asked, "do you still want to see what I'm working with?"

"Hell yeah! Hell yeah!" Lil' Shorty said as Peaches started dancing and taking her clothes off at the same time. When she was out of her jogging suit she still had her red and white thong and red top on. She was wearing it to the fullest.

"Damn Girl you making me fall for your sexy ass," Shorty said as he pulled out a rubber and handed it to Peaches. She opened it and put the tip of it in her mouth as she grabbed his hips. She got on her knees and led his penis into her mouth.

"Oh whew!" Shorty yelled.

She stopped sucking and asked, "what?"

"Oh nothing like that it just feel so good. I'm needing this baby," Shorty said as she continued for a minute. He laid her down and got to pounding her pussy just like she liked it. When they finished she was satisfied with both of her highs and she went back home.

---KQP---

"Damn Poochie you left us here like we was together!" Kim said.

"I thought y'all were cool people my fault," Poochie responded.

# Chapter Twelve

*Carmen*

"Girl last night was off the chain, but we had fun like a muthafucka," Carmen said to Tara as they sat in *Ladies First* hair salon.

"Yeah I had fun too. I thought about dancing all last night. I had pictured myself up on that stage doing my thang. I was hype like crazy. Muthafuckas was hollering and screaming my stage name!" Tara said.

"Stage name!" Carmen said smiling.

"Yeah I'm using Cupcake," Tara replied.

"What!"

"Cupcake!" Tara repeated, "I was feeling myself until Anthony ass woke me up and said stop making all that noise. I must have been talking in my sleep 'cause he straight woke me up. I'm gonna dance though."

"I'm gonna call around and see if I can hook you up with something."

"I sure hope they make it rain on this ass!" Tara said shaking her ass.

"Girl you crazy … Cupcake! Can you get my head started 'cause a bitch do got shit to do today!" Wanda said laughing.

"Don't y'all start calling me Cupcake up in here. This is a place of business," Tara said laughing.

"I got you though. Did you see how the whole day went? Be-Be and Cream got into it, then how all them project niggas got to rumbling. Both sides. Then how the three dudes were gone off the water (PCP) before we were leaving. I was sitting in the car. I see one of the three dudes laying on the ground. People was walking over him!" Carmen said.

"Straight up!" Tara said surprised.

"What y'all gonna do about the party bus? If y'all want to go to Detroit I need three grand to rent it for the whole weekend," Kay-Kay spoke up.

"How much you got?" Carmen asked.

"I got half," Kay-Kay responded.

"Well I got half and then some." Kay-Kay said, "I really want help on the other shit."

"Let me know what we need and I got the rest," Carmen said.

"Did Cream and Cody hook up yesterday?" Woo asked.

"Oh yeah, I don't care if they get salty or not. I don't want Be-Be in here trying to tear my shit up!" Carmen said.

"So what we got going on tonight?" Gail asked.

"I'll probably never get out of here tonight," Kay-Kay said.

"Since it's Saturday, let's go down to the flats and kick it," Carmen said.

"I haven't been in the flats in so long. I don't even know how to get down there," Gail replied.

"Well I went downtown and in the flats last week and I had a good time," Carmen said.

"See y'all don't really know the flats like I do. Back in the day," Carmen said.

"All shit here we go!" Bay-Bay said.

"Naw for real we use to stay in the flats and downtown. The Club 48, The Mirage, Metropolis … Top of the Flats. There was something down there jumping every night!" Carmen said, "I went out my way to make it down there at least three times a week."

"Girl do it still be jumping on Saturday nights?" Tara asked, "I don't even got nothing to wear while I'm talking about going out."

"Well, if you trying to kick it, then you better have something sexy to wear," Carmen said.

"That's why I got to strip 'cause I got to get my paper up," Tara said.

"I know that's right 'cause you haven't bought lunch yet!" Bay-Bay said laughing.

"You need to shut up 'cause you bumming a ride from me. Laugh at me for forgetting to pick you up!" Tara said.

"Hey y'all!" Cream said as she came through the door, "what everybody looking at me for?"

"Girl you something else," Kay-Kay said, "where Cody at?"

"I dropped him off right before I came here," Cream replied. Everybody started laughing.

"What?" Cream inquired, "I told you I wanted to have a lil' fun and that's what I did and girl that nigga was off the chain. We had a good time, y'all see I need a touch up."

"I got you!" Gail said.

"Yeah after I left from here yesterday, I went and got me some low riding *True Religion* jeans and a white *True Religion* shirt and I bought Cody some *Jordans,* a *Polo* shirt and jeans from Dillard's and we went and got something to eat from Chipotles in the Steelyard. We got some weed and some drinks and we went back to the hotel," Cream continued.

"What hotel?" Gail asked.

"Girl you know I stayed at the Holiday Inn Presidential suite," Cream answered.

"Girl you got money like that to blow!" Tara said while putting a lady under the dryer.

"Y'all think I'm not gonna get me no money and y'all doing what y'all do when y'all want to do what cha do. I can't be like this!" Tara said.

"Well I thought you got used to it!" Bay-Bay said.

"Bay-Bay shut the fuck up, 'cause soon as I come up your ass is gonna be right there wanting me to buy you something!" Tara said laughing.

"Oh I get money myself!" Bay-Bay said.

"Yeah cleaning the roof, equipment and taking out the trash!" Tara said.

"I do store runs and go get lunches too!" Bay-Bay said laughing, "I'm saying, I do get money though."

"Y'all talking about all this money talk. What y'all got on this party bus?" Kay-Kay asked.

"I thought y'all been talked about that money," Tara said laughing.

"We did, but I still need y'all that's going to come on in with y'all money," Kay-Kay replied.

"How much y'all need?" Cream asked.

"We need about $1500 to cover everything," Kay-Kay asked.

"Well I'm bringing my new friend Cody so I got a stack on it," Cream said smiling.

"I need me some weed," Carmen said.

"Where it's at?" Cream asked.

"I'll show you when I take me a lunch break in about fifteen minutes," Carmen replied.

*Ring Ring Ring* ... Carmen's phone rang.

"Hello?" she answered.

*"What's up baby?"* Montana asked.

"Nothing I'm just sitting here after doing six heads straight," Carmen replied.

*"Is you tired?"* he asked.

"Yeah a little bit, since you tried to keep me up all last night," Carmen said.

*"Shit after seeing all them asses and titties last night at Len Rocks I was thirsty as fuck for you, my fault I kept you up!"* Montana said.

"Boo I'm about to take my lunch break," Carmen told Montana, "I'll call you when I get through."

*"Come home real quick,"* Montana said laughing.

"Naw boyee your freaky self," Carmen said hanging up.

After hanging up Carmen and Cream got in Carmen's black convertible 2012 Saab. The sun was shining hard. Carmen let the top down.

Soon as she pulled up to the red light a white Tahoe with three guys in it looked down and hollered out the window asking Carmen and Cream if they were single and if they wanted to have some fun. Carmen instantly shot them down saying she was married, but Cream started fucking with them saying she wanted to kick it giving them a fake number. She lifted her shirt up and showed them her titties and that had them going. They followed Carmen's car three more lights then they turned down E. 40th Street.

"Girl you crazy!" Carmen said.

"YOLO!" Cream said.

"What?" Carmen asked.

"YOLO ... You only live once and I'm going to always do what I do!" Cream replied.

Carmen pulled up in the Longwood parking lot.

"Aye who got that good Kush?" Carmen asked a young dude on a bike.

"I got you baby girl," another dude overhearing her said and rushed to her car.

"What's this?" Carmen asked as he handed her two dimes of reggie bush weed.

"Naw baby! I'm looking for that good not no garbage!" Carmen said handing him his sacks back. When the other guy came back to the car he had several sacks of Kush varying in different prices.

"Let me get two twenties," Carmen said handing the guy two twenties from her purse and grabbing the sacks and smelling them.

"This is what I'm looking for," Carmen said. Cream grabbed a shell and put some Kush inside and rolled it up. Carmen drove out the parking lot and headed towards E. 55th Street to go to Mr. Hero's sub sandwich shop.

By the time they got there the Kush had kicked in and they had the munchies. They ordered two sandwiches each plus curly fries, cheesecake and some large sodas. They sat in the parking lot of the restaurant eating their food and laughing at everything that went past.

Carmen stopped laughing and asked Cream, "what are you really doing up here in Cleveland, Ohio?"

Cream laughed and played dumb at first until Carmen asked her again. Then she answered her question with a question of her own.

"Why? What you trying to get down?" Cream asked.

"You from Cali and we're trying to eat from out that way. We need a connect. I know you're getting money and I'm trying to get paper too. I know it takes money to make money. I got paper I just need the way. Turn me on to what you know," Carmen said looking dead serious at Cream.

"Look I can get you hooked up from out my way for 13 to 17 stacks per kilo. Thirteen if you come to Cali and 17 stacks if they got to bring it to you." Cream told Carmen.

"I been trying to find a plug in Cali, but I don't know how we can put it together. I got to run everything past my dude and see how he'll look at it and I'll let you know what's up the next time we talk," Carmen said.

"Listen Carmen don't ever talk no drugs to me over the phone. I don't care what's it's about," Cream said.

"I feel that," Carmen replied.

"So what you got planned today?" Carmen asked Cream.

"Well I'm about to go and get something to wear for today. It's hot today so I might get me a sundress," Cream responded.

*Ring Ring Ring* … "Hold on," Cream said answering her phone, "Hello?"

*"Hey there baby. How are you doing?"* a man on the phone said.

"Oh I'm fine," Cream answered.

*"Are you back home?"* the man asked.

"Naw, I'm still in Cleveland. I'll be back home this Monday," Cream answered.

*"Are you okay?"* he asked Cream.

"I'm okay," she said, "but I can use some more money. I blew through the $5000 I brought with me. So yeah send me two more stacks and I'll be cool."

"Okay baby. I'll see you Monday," Cream said hanging up the phone.

"My fault," Cream said, "they miss Ms. Kitty." Cream said and they started laughing.

"Who was that?" Carmen asked.

"Oh that's one of my men," Cream answered.

"Girl you something else," Carmen said.

"I make it do what it do," Cream said laughing.

"Let's smoke another blunt before we go back to the shop," Carmen said.

"Carmen your ass is going to have to get a shop out in Cali when you get your money up all the way up, 'cause I be wanting my shit done like this out west," Cream said rolling the blunt up.

"That's what's up for sure. I want a chain of *Ladies First* salons without a doubt," Carmen said as she pulled up in front of her salon. They sat there and smoked the blunt then walked towards the shop.

"What's up Carmen?" one of the guys standing outside the shop said.

"Hey Meechie. Don't be running my customers off," Carmen said.

"Oh you know we're gonna take care of you and your peoples Carmen. What's Montana number? Call him and tell him that I'm trying to get with him," Meechie said.

"Okay," Carmen said walking into the shop.

"Damn y'all feeling y'allselves. Y'all ain't bring us nothing back?" Tara asked.

"Oh I forgot, it's food left in the car."

"Bay ... Bay ... Bay!" everybody said at once.

"I'm not Mr. Belvedere. Why y'all calling my muthafucking name!" Bay-Bay said.

"Well could you go get that food for me," Tara said.

---KQP---

"I can't wait until this day is over with," Kay-Kay said as she walked outside next door to the store.

"Do y'all have some rollers for ponytails?" Kay-Kay asked the clerk.

"Nope, we'll have some next week," he said.

"Well let me get three blunt shells and a pack of Newports," Kay-Kay She got her stuff, paid for it and walked back next door to the shop. When she walked in Carmen was putting a customer under the dryer saying her and Cream was going out for drinks that night.

Kay-Kay asked her where she was gonna go 'cause she heard that Club Sin was jumping downtown and it was a lot of ballers and dope boys that was going to be there.

"We can go down there 'cause I'm trying to catch up with Kyrie Irving that play for the Cavs," Cream said.

"I'll have my way with his fine ass," Bay-Bay jumped in saying.

"Me too girl! Well we can roll down there, but I wanted to go to the Dawg Pound, that's where all the ballers be for real," Gail said.

*Ring Ring Ring* … "Excuse me y'all. Hello?" Carmen answered her phone, "baby what's up? I got some information for you," Carmen said.

*"I hope it's good,"* Montana said on the other end of the call.

"It is," Carmen told him, "Okay I'll talk to you when I get off."

# Chapter Thirteen

## Montana

Montana woke up to find himself laying by himself. He looked at the clock and it was 12:17pm.

"Damn!" he said as he rolled over and grabbed his phone to check his calls. It was six calls missed. He instantly started calling them back. He dialed the 432 number back knowing it was Lil' Shorty. Lil' Shorty picked up on the 4th ring.

"Hello what's good nephew?" Montana said.

*"Nothing much, I called you last night to let you know I'm ready for you to fall back through,"* Lil' Shorty said in code letting Montana know he was finish with his package.

"Oh yeah that's what's up. I'll be down there after I get dressed," Montana said as he thought about how Lil' Shorty was taking care of business.

"Neph can you handle more?" Montana asked. Shorty thought about the come up he was about to get blessed with and said, *"hell yeah!"*

"Well I'll be down there in a little while," Montana said hanging up the phone. Montana called Mack next.

*"Hello?"* Mack answered.

"What's up my nigga?" Montana asked.

*"Aw it ain't nothing to it. What's up with you?"*

"I'm about to get up and out after I get dressed."

*"Man I wound up fucking Kim all last night. We all played in the shower for a minute. When me and Kim got in the bed waiting on Poochie she put her shit on and left us in the house. So I pounded Kim's pussy out until we got tired and went to sleep."*

"What she say about the one shit?"

*"Oh we got some holler, but I'll tell you about that when you come and get me."*

"Where she at?" Montana asked.

*"Poochie is at home and Kim is at her hotel. Poochie was outside until about 4:30am so she probably still sleeping."*

"Straight up? What she say she was doing out that late?"

*"She say she needed some air. So I rolled with it plus Kim was there so I got to fuck and talk with her."*

"Look Mack, I'm about to go get ready now. I'll call you when I'm on my way."

*"Alright big homie, I'll see you when you get here,"* Mack said ending the call. Montana hung up and made a few more calls.

He got his clothes out the closet and ran him some bathwater. He went in his bedroom and pulled several bags out of his floor safe, plus the bag he got that night. He poured them all out on his bed.

*Damn,* he thought to himself smiling as he waited for the water to fill up in the tub. He started separating the bills apart. Most of the them were 100's, 50's and 20's, but there were still a lot of tens and fives. He estimated it to be around 90 stacks. He pulled his other bag out and opened it up. It had two large bags and one small bag inside of it. *That's two and half kilos,* he thought to himself as he walked in the bathroom to take his bath.

*Damn,* he thought about the stuff he wanted out of life as he got dressed. He put on a *True Religion* outfit and a fresh pair of new *Timberland* boots. After counting the money and dope, he put it back in the floor board spot that he specially made. He stopped and went back to the stash spot and grabbed the bag of dope. He grabbed a large bag and the half full bag of powder and put it in a tennis shoe box and put the box back in the shoe bag, making it look like a pair of shoes. He walked outside and put the bag in the trunk of his car. The day was starting to get busy and the sun had everybody out and about. Montana was no different.

*Ring Ring Ring* … was the sound he heard as he cut the music down in his car.

*"Hello,"* Mack said as Montana answered his phone.

"Aye I'm outside in front of your house," Montana said

*"Come in so we can talk,"* Mack said. As Montana got out his car he heard a horn blow at him. He turned around and it was Quincy. Montana waved at him as he rode past then he grabbed the bag out of his trunk and walked in Mack's apartment. Mack opened the door and Montana walked in and sat down at the table, sitting the bag right next to him.

"Mack I need you to cook all this shit up for me," Montana said opening the bag and box that he had the kilo and a half in.

"Damn you putting all this down," Mack said.

"Yeah man it's time to start turning this shit up my nigga."

"I got you," Mack said grabbing the bag. Mack went and grabbed the equipment to put the work together and instantly got to putting his magic down making two whole kilos of crack.

"Mack?" Montana said his name getting his attention, "what Kim say?"

"Oh yeah, she told me her people got that work at a good price. Depending on what we're spending and how we get it."

"What you mean and say?"

"I told her we'll spend a hundred stacks for five of them thangs (kilos) and we'll pay $110.000 if they get them brought to us and $90,000 if we have to go get them ourselves."

"I ain't tripping one way or another though. Well hopefully she can have them bring them to us." Montana said thinking of the deal he would be getting if he gets them at that price.

"I ain't gonna lie if we have to go to Miami then it is what it is. I'm not tripping." Montana said while Mack pulled the work out of the microwave and started stirring it around.

"Montana man that hoe Kim was thirsty as fuck for Poochie last night. She was all on me too, like all hoes be," Mack said, "but she wanted to fuck Poochie and the way Poochie pulled out, I don't know if she really like girls, but I'm definitely gonna have her put it on Kim to see if we can get shit at a better price," Mack said while still mixing, stirring and cooking the work.

"You're putting it down on this shit!" Montana said watching Mack do what he does. Mack handed him a coffee jar with the whole bottom filled with cooked coke.

"That's a kilo," Mack said pouring the whole other large bag in the pot.

"I been going at nephew and he been taking care of his business. So I'm gonna throw him the half." Mack gave him a look.

"I'm about to turn it all the way up. I'm giving him a chance to see if he ready or not. With this half of key. It's no looking back for most people," Montana said as Mack handed Montana the second jar and put the last of the dope in the pot.

"I got all the love in the world for Shorty and I hope he can handle it," Mack said thinking back at the time he fronted Lil' Shorty an ounce and Shorty fucked the money up.

"I know you probably thinking he'll fuck up," Montana said, "but I'm gonna risk it, plus the way you're bringing back all these extra grams, I'll have a half a key extra anyway."

"Know that's right!" Mack said still stirring the coke.

"You got that for show, you know that you got to hit the Compound and King Kennedy up on this shit. I been getting hit up like a muthafucka since we went out last night," Mack said.

"That's what's up 'cause I got to come down on all my lil' niggas on Case Court and in Longwood," Montana said.

"Oh yeah, you want that last one I got right?" Montana said referring to the kilo.

"Yeah I need that for sure," Mack said still stirring the coke up.

"Aye Montana, I'm trying to get this paper up. I had played around long enough. I'm like you, I want more out of life, than a car or jewelry. I want to pave a way for the future," Mack said.

"I feel that, that's why from here on we're about to go up. If you say what you mean, because I myself feel good about everything I'm doing right now and I know I got a vision to know where I'm going and where I want to be. I'm in it to win it and I'm gonna come up for sure," Montana said.

"That's what I'm talking about. Let's get this finished so we can go get this money," Mack said.

"Aye Mack call Kim and tell her I need to holler at her and I want to see her soon," Montana said.

"I'll call her now," Mack said calling her and telling her what Montana said.

"Hello Kim," Mack said.

*"Yeah,"* Kim answered.

"Aye this Montana, Mack told me y'all talked and I want to talk to you myself and see what's up. Where are you at?" Montana asked.

*"I'm downtown at my hotel room,"* Kim said.

"Well can you meet us over Poochie's house in 20 minutes?" Montana asked her.

*"I'm getting dressed, so yeah I can make it. Is Poochie over there?"* Kim asked as she was putting on her clothes she bought from the mall the day before.

"Naw but I'll see you when you get there," Montana said.

Mack finished cooking the work up. They bagged it up and they were on their way to Poochie's house.

"Montana where that good at?" Mack asked.

"You know I got that shit in the armrest, but we got that shit in the trunk. That's the only reason why I haven't fired that shit up yet," Montana said as he drove to Poochie's apartment.

"It's been a long time since we seen the sun shining like this," Mack said, "I see us going where the days are shining more and more."

"Like me!" Montana said laughing and thinking about the future to be.

When he pulled up in Poochie's parking lot in Longwood. There were a group of young Longwood niggas standing over by the playground area. A few of them were making sales on the crack side, but most of them was selling weed in all different quantities and qualities.

One of the young dudes named Bus asked Montana, "what's good OG?" As he walked past them going to a weed customer sitting in a parked car. When they walked past the group one of the young guys asked Montana if he had some work for $600. Montana left Mack walking alone as he responded to the young dude.

"Hit me up in 20 minutes and I'll serve you for your money," Montana said. Mack knocked on Poochie's door and waited for her to answer.

"Who is it?" Poochie asked responding to the knock on the door.

"It's us baby," Mack said as she opened the door and let them in, closing the door behind them.

"Hey y'all," she said giving Montana a hug and giving Mack a hug and kiss.

"What y'all up to?" she asked. She offered them something to eat.

"Yeah! Hell yeah!" they both yelled at the same time.

"I'll cook some chicken and French fries for y'all Poochie said as she walked in the kitchen. She had on some thin pajama pants that made her ass bounce as she walked.

"Damn baby that ass looking good," Mack said as he followed her into the kitchen squeezing her ass a few times.

He looked at Montana and said, "this right here got Kim going. She gone come in." Steady squeezing Poochie's round, soft ass.

"I see you missed me huh!" Poochie said seeing Montana out the corner of her eye sneaking a peek at her ass. Knowing what she was doing.

She bent over to grab a skillet out the bottom cabinet. Her legs were spread wide open as she bent straight over in front of him making it look like a doggy style position.

*Damn* Montana thought as the doorbell rang and shook him out of his freaky thoughts.

"Who is it?" Mack asked.

"It's Kim!" she said as Poochie asked Montana why they left and did they enjoy the show last night.

"Shit I had to go before some shit got started, but I enjoyed myself for show. You did your thing. Shake what yo momma gave ya!" Montana said laughing as Kim and Mack came in the kitchen.

"Hey y'all!" Kim said giving Montana a hug then seductively giving Poochie one.

"Girl you showed your ass both ways last night," Kim said as they all started laughing.

"Where your ass go last night?" Kim asked.

"Shit that dancing had my stomach burning up inside and I needed some air!" Poochie said as she pulled the chicken and fries out their skillets.

"Kim you want some of this food?" Seeing what it was and knowing Poochie made it Kim said, "hell yeah!"

After they all sat down and ate Montana said, "excuse me let me holler at you Kim." Mack and Poochie walked in the living room and sat on the couch. Montana instantly got to asking what was up with her people and how long would it take for them to meet up and talk about the business.

Kim told him that he could catch the plane back to Miami with her and things could get going soon as possible. Montana thought about it to himself as he called Mack into the living room and told him what the deal was about going to Miami. Mack got pumped up 'cause he knew that if they get a Miami plug then shit was gonna be on and popping.

"That's what's up!" Mack said as he walked back in the kitchen and told Poochie he was going to Miami.

"I want to go," Poochie said, "I want to go meet *Uncle Luke from the 2 Live Crew* while I'm down there."

"This is a business trip. When we go again I'll let you go with us," Mack was telling her until Montana said, "we can let her and Carmen go with us when we go."

Poochie jumped in the air saying, "ain't no mystery, we're about to go hard in Miami!" She was giving everybody hugs as she went upstairs to get her clothes together.

"Damn Montana how you know I ain't want no Miami pussy?" Mack said as Kim spoke up saying, "you already had some," rubbing her coochie smiling.

"We need some decoys while we're down there anyway. That's why we need our girls to roll with us, playa," Montana said as he pulled out his phone to call Carmen.

# Chapter Fourteen

## *Lil' Shorty*

Lil' Shorty had just got up. He went in his closet and got the black duffle bag which contained all the money he made the day before. As he started counting it up he thought about what he was gonna do with it. He counted everything he made and it came up to $14, 675. Though he owed Montana eight stacks for the work. He smiled at the fact he made six thousand and some change extra.

*Damn* he thought thinking about what Peaches told him about the connect and the people she knew. He started putting together a master plan to come up.

*Ring Ring Ring* ... He heard his phone go off as he snapped back to reality. Answering the phone and still stacking the money in stacks of $1,000's.

*"What's going on Lil' Shorty?"* Skeet asked.

"Aw I don't know nothing now. What's good homie," Lil' Shorty said recognizing his ole school friend's voice.

*"Are you up and about yet?"* Skeet asked him.

"Naw I'm just getting out of bed, but you know I move for that paper," Lil' Shorty said, "what's up?"

*"Don't nothing come to a sleeper but a dream,"* Skeet said.

"I know."

*"Well when you get up and about, I need you to come up to the bar and holla at me. I got a lil' money for you if you want it,"* Skeet said knowing the word money would get him up.

"Soon as I take care of my hygiene and things. I'll swing past there," Lil' Shorty said as he thought about what Skeet wanted.

Skeet used to be hustling back in the day before he fell on an eight to 25-year stretch. He caught a robbery, assault, kidnapping and drug case. That was all over a dude that he fronted some dope to. The dude he fronted the dope to didn't pay him his money. He went to his house and kicked his door down and beat the man up very badly and took the lil' money and drugs he had left. The police caught him on the scene. He was lucky after the chase he took the police on that involved 12 police cars.

That was only half of it. The other half was while he was in jail, the so called friend he had, knocked his baby mama off and they took his money. They took all his shit and ran off on him. After that he started busting checks and running after hour bootleg joints, which made him money but slow money.

Every now and again he'll have guys from back in the day wanting drugs and if he could make a quick flip without the static, he sometimes would chance it and this was one of those times.

Lil' Shorty got his self together and started cleaning his spot up when his phone started ringing.

*"Hello nephew,"* Montana said.

"What's up!" Lil' Shorty replied.

*"I'm outside, open the door for me."* Montana said on the other end.

"I got you!" Lil' Shorty said while going towards the door unlocking it and letting Montana in with a large bag in his hand. Montana gave Lil' Shorty dap and a hug. He made his way to the kitchen table with Lil' Shorty right behind him.

"Nephew look here. I'm gonna tell you this here before we get to doing anything heavy. This life is real. I mean it's a life to come up off of, but this here is a life that could have you in the joint forever and me too. I'm willing to put everything I live for on the line for this opportunity. You could do better than me. I'm telling you this to let you know that you got that choice to choose before I give you anything else. Are you in our out?"

"I'm in!" Lil' Shorty said as Montana told him about how now was the time to come up and he was upping his supply to a half a kilo.

"Do your thang but, be careful."

"Damn!" Lil' Shorty said as he looked at the 18 hard ounces of crack.

"What? You can't handle this?"

"Hell yeah! I was just saying I'm about to kill them with $25 rocks," Lil' Shorty said as he grabbed the package and went right to work chopping ounce for ounce up in bricks.

"Unc?"

"What's good neph?"

"You know I got that paper from that other shit."

"Straight up? What you got?"

"It's $14,000 and some change."

"That's what's up you keep that. Get you a safe 'cause if you're going to hustle like you are then you're about to be loaded." Montana said smiling while walking out to his car.

Lil' Shorty jumped in the air and said, "I'm about to be on!"

He locked the door and went back to the kitchen where he had some of the bagged up crack sitting on the table. He grabbed his razor and finished cutting up the ounces of crack. After that he grabbed his phone and started calling all the people he knew that sold and smoked and told them that he had enough to serve everybody what they wanted in rocks.

When he finished, he knew he had to look the part, so he put on a navy blue *Roca Wear* sweat suit and some blue and white Air Max's and a wife beater t-shirt. He grabbed his chain and threw it around his neck as he walked out the house to the Case Court strip.

At 4:30 pm Case Court was already jumping. There were so many people just waiting for somebody to come outside with some crack and that somebody was Lil' Shorty. A few people spotted Lil' Shorty walking down the street. Candy Gurl knew not to yell his name, so she like the rest of the crowd waited until he got there. He got to the crowd of people and they went off.

"Shorty I got …" he heard as he pulled a Ziploc bag full of rocks out his draws saying, "y'all line up."

"I got $25 rocks that's it! Now y'all line up and let me know what y'all want," he said in a stern voice.

"Let me get one," Another man said handing shorty a twenty and a ten, then a lady said, "can I get five for a hundred?" While swinging her arms back and forth.

"Hell naw!" Lil' Shorty said, then saying to the crowd, "I got $25 rocks no deals, so don't ask!" Lil' Shorty said as he served the crowd and stuffed his pockets with all the cash he made.

"Lil' Shorty let me holla at you," CB said as Shorty stood on the porch in front of the apartment complex.

"Come mere," Lil' Shorty said calling him up on the porch.

"Short I got two stacks I'm trying to spend with you," CB said.

"That's what's up!" Shorty said. He told CB that he could only give him an extra $200 worth of rocks because his rocks were so big and that he was going to already make a profit by breaking his rocks down. Besides that, nobody had his good product anyway and if he keep working with him he'll put an extra hundred every time he came back.

That was right up his alley 'cause CB was worth a key. He just didn't have a hook but now with what Lil' Shorty said he had a plug. He instantly thought about buying all his dope out every time Shorty would let him. He copped the two stacks and walked off.

Old Man James walked up and told Lil' Shorty that the Compound was dry just as he was about to walk over there and tell everybody he had dope.

Lil' Shorty served a few more people.

He walked towards Longwood Apartments. When he got in the Wood, on the side of the building there was a group of dudes shooting dice, selling bud and water. As he walked up he touched the side of his waist making sure he had his pistol right where it needed to be. Not because he wasn't loved and respected. That's just how it was in the bricks and though he put in work over the years, he still had to be careful outside down the way because the youngens was growing up and putting in work on call.

It didn't matter if you were tough, had money or paved the way. If they felt, they wanted something you had, then they were coming at you with them big guns. They were always carrying on them and it was nothing to see an illegal act at any moment while being there.

Lil' Shorty lived the life and he didn't fear or bar nothing. He was on whatever the situation called for, but now he was about his paper, so there he was posted up in LA. He told the people that sold crack about his hustle and how he wanted to do things.

He got a lil' team together and told them about coming up and he wanted them to come up with him. He gave about five people $500 in rocks and they were to bring back $400 each. After doing that Lil' Shorty did the same thing in the Compound, Unwin and in King Kennedy. He knew if he could put the locks in all the projects he fucked with, then he was gonna come up for sure and that's what he wanted to do.

Lil' Shorty sold out and went back to his apartment. He took another bath and put some fresh gear on. He liked the *True Religion* outfit he bought from the booster chic Crazy T. She was a chic that grew up in the bricks that made her living off of boosting clothes. It's been said that going into Crazy T's apartment was like stepping into Dillard's in the mall and everyone in the bricks knew if you needed an outfit Crazy T's spot was where you went if you wanted to pay half the price of Dillard's.

Lil' Shorty felt good with the hook up he had on. After getting dressed Shorty went in his room and grabbed his bud out of his jacket pocket. He felt he was finally getting something together as he rolled his blunt up and lit it. He coughed a few times as he picked up his phone and called some of his friends and told them he was out and about.

Mikey told Lil' Shorty he had four hundred he wanted to spend before he left. Lil' Shorty told him that he was gonna sale him $400 worth and front him $400 worth on consignment. Lil' Shorty grabbed the bag he was putting money in and poured it on the table. He sold a lot of his crack and some he fronted out, but he still made several stacks and still had a big bag half way full of crack. He grabbed some crack out and put it in another bag.

Skeet had been texting him telling him that if he wanted to make the sale he better hurry up 'cause his dude was ready to leave and go somewhere else.

Lil' Shorty went outside and went to his '87 Monte Carlo SS. He knew he wanted something else since he first got the car from Montana. Now that he was making money, a car was the first thing on his list to get when he started buying stuff. Even though the Monte Carlo still got him where he wanted to go. Lil' Shorty was tired of the rusted car. He put his drugs under the tire in his trunk and got in and pulled out.

As he rode down Case Court and around the bend to Outhwaite he noticed a navy blue Tahoe coming up behind him blowing the horn. As he pulled over he saw Mikey behind the driver's seat. Mikey jumped out and came up on to Lil' Shorty's window saying, "damn nigga you gonna leave me."

"Naw man I was gonna call you when I got to where I'm going," Lil' Shorty said, "Mikey follow me up to Skeet's spot," Shorty continued as he rolled up his window and pulled out with Mickey following behind him.

When Lil' Shorty got to Skeet's the parking lot was halfway empty. Most of the people wasn't coming out until the chics came out and that was around 10:30pm, but Lil' Shorty liked that it was still early because that meant he had time to sale his shit and get ready for the chics to fall in without him missing a beat.

Lil' Shorty and Mikey walked in Skeet's bar to the loud music of *Yo Gotti*. Though the spot wasn't packed, there were still a few cuties in the building. Lil' Shorty told Mikey to order some drinks. He seen Skeet and another dude walking to the back. Skeet introduced them to each other while hugging Lil' Shorty.

"Damn you looking good!" Skeet told Lil' Shorty.

"Well you know money have anybody looking good. Look at your ugly ass!" Lil' Shorty said laughing.

"Nigga fuck you!" Skeet said still laughing.

"What's good though?" Lil' Shorty asked pulling the large bag of rocks out.

"Holla at him," Skeet told Big Blue.

"Do you want to sell me that whole bag?" Big Blue asked.

"Yeah I'll sell it to you but I want rock for rock worth," Lil' Shorty said. Big Blue was looking at the extras off the top and he copped the whole package and asked Lil' Shorty if he had some more. Lil' Shorty gave him his number and told him he had whatever he wanted. Lil' Shorty got the money and gave both of them dap.

Lil' Shorty walked back in front of the spot. Mikey had ordered the drinks and had two chics sitting with him. When Mikey noticed Lil' Shorty walking up, he introduced him to the two chics named Nicole and Shawnti. They were some chics he grew up with in the projects.

After sitting and talking to the ladies over a few drinks, Lil' Shorty said his goodbyes and he and Mikey left Skeet's bar and drove downtown to the flats. They rode past all the spots' parking lots pimping.

"I'm about to finish getting my paper," Lil' Shorty told Mikey as he followed him back down the way.

# Chapter Fifteen

## *Carmen*

*Ring Ring Ring* … "Hello, where you at boo?" Carmen asked Montana as she pulled up to the driveway of their house.

*"I'm sitting right here in the backyard of the house,"* Montana answered.

"Doing what?" Carmen asked.

*"Playing with Kilo and Kush,"* Montana answered.

"You love them dogs," Carmen said talking about the pit bulls he had bought. Kilo was an all-white muscle bound boy and Kush was a grey girl. They both was starting to become well trained. Besides all the time Montana stayed in the streets hustling, he trained his dogs, plus for the past eight months he had them K-9 schooled.

At first Carmen wasn't really on dogs until about three months ago somebody tried to walk her in the house to rob her. That's when she yelled "watcha," which was the word that meant attack to them and they came out their backroom doing just that to the last man standing of the two guys. Ever since then, they were her best friends and she start loving them.

As she got out of the car Kilo and Kush ran to her jumping in the air and barking showing her they were happy. She walked over to Montana and gave him a kiss. She then grabbed his blunt out the ashtray and puffed it a few times and sat it back down and walked in the house. Montana followed her with the dogs right behind him.

She turned around and said, "babe, I talked to Cream and she was saying her people had kilos for 15 stacks and 17 stacks if they bring them to us."

"Oh yeah, well I talked to Kim and we're going to Miami tomorrow," Montana responded.

"Straight up!" Carmen said as she walked up the stairs.

Carmen had become a nice young lady at only 27 years old. She lived a life that forced her into the streets at the tender age of 12 years old. That's when crack caught up to her household and everybody in it, which included her mother, grandmother, aunt and uncle.

They all had caught the vapors and started smoking up everything they could. Shit got so tight back then that her aunt sold a pair of her favorite jeans, which left her with one pair for the rest of the school year.

There were plenty of nights Carmen and her little brother Tone would go to sleep hungry. She remembered going to steal packs of lunch meat from the plaza grocery store. By the time she was 14 years old her body had filled out so good that guys older than her used to try and run game on her saying that they would do this and that for her. They ran all the game that any young chic would go for, but Carmen held out on sex, which made dudes want her even more.

They use to come to her house every day trying to get in her pants. She started seeing how giving a little attention would have dudes doing whatever she wanted. Everything was going right up her alley until she met June. June was a dope boy who was always fly on the clothes side. He bought all the latest things out and Carmen liked that. She gave June a chance and that's all it took. June put the rush on her making her fall in love in no time.

June flipped and started dogging her. He made her do things she didn't want to do, but she did them for him. June started setting her out with his Outlaws and whoever else he wanted her to sleep with. Carmen was a fool in love.

---KQP---

Carmen sat on her bed trying to remember some of the numbers to the gentlemen clubs she used to work at. She remembered she told Tara and Poochie that she would call around to see if she could put them on with some decent spots to dance at. She called Melrose, then Secrets, which were full, but on the strength that Carmen was good people, both spots told her to bring the ladies in.

After that Carmen started getting a few things together. She knew she would probably have to shop while she was in Miami, so she just started putting Montana's things together.

Carmen's phone went off and she picked it up. *You have a collect call from Tone. An inmate at the Mansfield Correctional Facility. If you wish to accept the call press one and hold,* the recorded message said as Carmen pressed one.

*"Hello!"* Tone said as the phone call connected.

"Hey there brother," Carmen said.

Tone began to talk, *"what's up sis? I haven't heard from you lately what's up?"*

"Nothing I been good," Carmen said, "what's up with you?"

*"They just up and told me I'm being released today,"* Tone said.

"Get the fuck outta here!" Carmen said, "when?"

*"Today!"* Tone said, *"I need a ride right now."*

"Swear!" Carmen said excitedly.

*"I'm going through process right now!"* Tone said.

"I'm coming to get you right now!" Carmen said hanging up the call.

Carmen called Montana, "babe!"

"What's up!" Montana answered.

"My brother being released from jail right now and we got to go pick him up!" Carmen said excitedly.

"Straight up! I thought he got denied at the board!" Montana said.

"He did but they're releasing him today and he need us to come and pick him up," Carmen said.

"Well what are we waiting for? We got to go get lil' bruh," Montana said thinking about back when he heard Lil' Tone was shooting at the police at the bottom of Case Court. The nigga had got bonded over from juvenile and copped to a 10 to 25 and after 12 years they were letting him go.

Carmen called damn near the whole family to let them know about Tone getting released and the trip they were about to take. After talking to the family she made reservations for roundtrip tickets from Cleveland to Miami for six people for the next day with American Airlines.

---KQP---

When they arrived at Mansfield prison, there were people waiting for their loved ones to be released and some were waiting to visit. Carmen went to the front counter and asked one of the correctional officers was a Antonie Walker ready to be picked up. Tone walked out wearing an all red jogging suit.

"Damn blood!" Montana said playing like he was a gang banger.

"What's up?" Tone asked hugging Carmen until she started crying saying how much she missed him. Tone gave Montana a hug too. He saw the lady CO named Ms. Jordan he wanted to fuck.

"Ms. Jordan what's good?" Tone asked as he walked out the prison to the car. Once he got in the car Tone said, "fire that shit up!"

Carmen asked him, "ain't you on parole?"

"Naw baby my shit maxed out. I can do whatever the fuck I want to do now, thanks to The Lane Decision, I'm free!" Tone said.

"Oh yeah that's good because we're going to Miami," Carmen said.

"I'm going!" Tone said.

"I already got us tickets," Carmen said as Tone sparked up the blunt Montana gave him.

"Boy you got to get out of that jogging suit," Carmen said. She told Montana to stop at the outlet store so they could buy Tone some clothes.

Once they got to the clothing outlet store Tone went crazy buying everything he wanted. He tried on about ten outfits and about six different pairs of tennis shoes. Tone was always a good dresser. He mixed and matched some nice *Polo* outfits together, then he put a few outfits of *True Religion* together as well. After putting those hook ups together, he went to the *Gucci* shop and bought a red and green *Gucci* shirt, some white cargo shorts and a pair of red and green *Gucci* tennis shoes. He knew he had to come correct. So he grabbed the hat, belt and neck bag. Carmen and Montana put a few things on the counter and paid the clerk for the clothes. Tone put an outfit on considering he was fresh out of the joint and he was glowing.

Soon as he stepped out of the dressing room the clerk was looking hard at him and Tone shot his shot, "aye what's up baby? Can I get to know you?" he asked the brown skinned chic with the low tapered haircut, colored honey blonde. She gave Tone her phone number and told him to call her.

Tone, Carmen and Montana walked out the store. When they got back in the car Tone sparked the blunt back up passing it around as he told Montana and Carmen about opening up a barbershop and pool hall once he got his paper up.

Montana told him about being up in the game and how he was about to come up if his move goes through like he planned it. Carmen knew the situation that was at hand and though she was down with her man, she also wanted the best for her little brother, well younger brother since Tone stood 6' 2" and weighed 215 lbs. and he had just got out of jail.

Carmen was gonna do her best to keep Tone out the way. She also knew that Tone was hard headed and a Taurus so she had to have a heart-to-heart to see what he really wanted to do.

They pulled off the freeway into Downtown Cleveland.

"You know that's the new casino right there," Carmen said as she pointed. They made a turn down Prospect Avenue headed towards the east side of Cleveland. Carmen, Montana and Tone went to *Ladies First* where Tone got cleaned up and retested his game by shooting his shot at Kay-Kay.

"As much as I'd like to take you home, you my girl lil' brother and I can't mix business with pleasure," Kay-Kay said as she walked over to her other customer and started her hair.

Carmen told everybody that she was going out of town for a few days and that the salon would be still open with Tara as acting manager. Tara told Carmen she wanted to go too until she told her about the two spots that wanted her to dance at that night and the next night. Tara told Carmen that she was scared but she needed the money.

"A scared bitch is a broke bitch!" Carmen said as they started laughing. Tara was hyping herself up for the debut she had coming up. She had already bought several outfits to wear. She had an all-white lace thong outfit with emerald colored rhinestones that spelled cupcake out in capital letters. She had dreamed about dancing several times. She needed the money for sure, but she wanted her own shit.

Though her and Carmen were good friends she envied Carmen. She thought of how Carmen had struggled growing up and how her life turned around for the better and that's what she wanted. A life for the better. She made a promise to herself that she was gonna come up. Carmen told Tara that she had what it took to get money. She also told her the ropes of dancing.

"No drinks, no drugs, it's all about dancing and keeping yourself respectable," Carmen told her.

# Chapter Sixteen

## *Montana*

"Carmen hurry up," Montana said as Carmen took her dear old time getting dressed. She and Montana was excited and ready to get to Miami. He stayed up all night making plans on what he wanted to do. He told Mack and Tone that he wanted them near when he made the deal. He had made sure that each one of them carried 25 stacks each which came up to $150,000.

He took an extra 50 stacks to play with considering Tone had just came home the day prior and wanted to welcome his new hook to some Cleveland flavor.

Montana finished getting his bits and pieces together. He called Mack and told him to make sure he, Poochie and Kim were ready to go 'cause Carmen had made the reservations for 10:15am and they were up and ready to go.

Mack told Montana that they were packed up and they were waiting for them to come and pick them up. When they all arrived at Hopkins Airport, Montana told everybody to make sure they didn't have nothing illegal on them. They all had money but he was talking about shit besides that. They carried their personal carryon bags that had their identification cards, an outfit, and a hygiene bag.

It was a while since Montana had been on a plane, but the last time he was on one he told himself that he was gonna fly the friendly skies and that is what he was doing. All six of them got in line to be searched. Carmen passed everyone their ticket to get on the plane.

Once they got on the plane they all got snacks to munch on. They listened to music from the airplane's IPods and enjoyed the flight to Miami. Montana looked out at the land beneath the clouds in the air as he looked across and told Mack and Tone that the sky was the limit and this was the time to do the damn thang. Mack and Tone agreed.

Tone asked Mack who was Poochie and Kim. He saw a Spanish looking chic walk past going towards the bathroom.

Tone yelled out, "what's up baby?" Montana noticed the chic and told Tone to lay low on her.

Tone looked around confused as Montana said, "that's a man!" Tone looked dumb and Montana and Mack both busted out laughing making Carmen, Poochie and Kim wonder what was going on.

The flight was quick. They landed in Miami International Airport in two and a half hours. The sun was shining and the day was already going. There was a lot of people waiting on flights as well as arriving to the smiles of their loved ones. Montana and his crew went to baggage claims to pick up their luggage while awaiting Kim's cousins Juan and Jose to pick them up. They all went to the food court and ordered food as they looked around the airport. There were a lot of restaurants and boutiques from all different people and cultures.

Montana walked over to a Cuban cigar stand and bought some cigars. Carmen, Poochie and Kim walked towards a Chanel shoe store with Kim leading the way. They went in and bought a few outfits and came back to the food court where Montana, Mack and Tone were eating some type of beef patties from the Haitians stand.

Hertz Rental car called Carmen's phone and told her that two cars were ready to be picked up. Carmen rented a Cadillac truck and a Cadillac STS for them to ride in while in Miami. Though they wanted to floss big, then wasn't the time.

Montana told himself as he thought of the vision he had in his mind about coming up. Just as he snapped back to reality two guys walked up and Kim jumped up.

"Aye y'all here go my people right here!" Kim said giving Juan and Jose hugs while introducing everyone to each other.

Montana sensed their vibe and knew by the way they carried themselves that he was finally meeting some people that was the real deal connects.

Montana and Mack jumped behind the wheels of the Caddies. They followed Juan who was showing them where they would be staying while in Dade County. Tone and Carmen was in Montana's car enjoying the sight of everything Miami had to offer. Tone was saying he couldn't wait until the night came so that they could go see the strippers Miami had.

Tone had heard stories about *Uncle Luke from 2 Live Crew* and how Miami had some of the baddest strippers and now that he was down there he wanted to see for himself.

He looked at the people that passed by and knew it had to be somewhat true because a lot of the women that passed them looked to be in great shape and sexy.

Montana asked Carmen about the Embassy Resort and she checked them in. They had three Presidential suites that was at the downtown beach front resort. She read the pamphlet that listed all the activities there was to do and all the entertainment places to go while at the resort.

Tone spoke up, "I want to go to the beach and ride some jet skis."

"That's what's up," Montana said, "but before we get into all that we got to make sure we get put on. This right here is a business trip, so know before anything we take care of business first."

Montana's phone rang as he waited at the light, he answered, "hello?"

Mack spoke up saying, *"this the life my nigga, I can get used to this down here."*

"I know that's right," Montana said.

He turned into the hotel parking lot saying, "we're here," as he hung up the phone. He parked a couple spots down from Juan and got out the car with Mack parking and getting out right in pursuit.

Jose looked at Montana and waved his hands in the air and said, "welcome to Miami!" He smiled at Montana while reaching out his hand for a handshake. Then he shook Mack's and Tone's hands while hugging Carmen and Poochie.

Juan spoke and said, "if y'all are friends of Kim then y'all are friends of ours. Our code is LRL Love Respect Loyalty," Juan continued, "that's everything we stand on, that's more than life to me."

Mack said, "me too."

Montana walked to the front desk where Carmen was getting the keys to the rooms. She gave Mack and Tone theirs and she held onto hers and Montana's. They all got on the elevator and went up to Montana's suite. When they reached the top floor, the elevator opened up into the front room of the suite. The room was burgundy and gold in color and it looked very expensive. The carpet was thick and burgundy with the drapes and furniture to match. There was a hot tub off to the left side by the bathroom.

The bedroom was toward the back of the suite with a patio that looked off to the beach. The view was great and with a pair of binoculars, you could see the inland of Cuba. The bedroom had a king-sized bed with a 60" Sony flat screen TV and a built in wall aquarium with tropical fish inside of it.

Montana told Carmen, Poochie and Kim that he wanted to talk to the fellas. They grabbed the keys to one of the Caddies and headed towards the elevators and left the suite.

Montana walked to the front room and cut the IPod on. *Young Jeezy* was playing *All White Everything* through the speakers as he walked back to the kitchen and sat at the table with Juan, Jose, Mack and Tone.

Montana spoke and said, "I would …" then restarted his sentence, "…we would like to do some business, if the coke is good and the prices are right, we'll keep coming back."

"What can y'all do to make us keep coming back?" Montana asked. Juan said he could let a kilo go for 17 stacks a piece here in Miami and 20 if they have to be sent to Cleveland. He assured Montana that the Coke would be a great quality. He opened a little caplet then handing it to Montana telling him to try it. Montana declined the offer and asked Mack to try it. Mack did a hit and it instantly rushed him and he gave the nod.

Montana looked at Juan and said, "it's on!"

After setting the deal up and going over the hows. Montana was satisfied with the deal and the arrangements he had got. He told Jose and Juan that he wanted to celebrate and get use to the Miami life. Jose told Montana that the life began on the beaches, so after getting everything together, Montana, Mack and Tone headed down to the beachfront to celebrate.

They went down there and it was just like they thought Miami would be. The beach was crowded with people. There were people tanning, swimming, playing volleyball, reading books and watching their kids playing all at the same time. Montana and his crew walked over to the beach bar and ordered bottles of Moet and Daiquiris as they sat at a table with an umbrella top. There were a lot of women walking past ordering drinks and having a good time with their pretty, sexy bikinis on. Though Montana was with Carmen, he still would shoot his shot every now and then to see if he still had the old game he used to have.

He asked a few ladies if they wanted some drinks as they sat at the table enjoying the whole scene. Miami was a lot different from Cleveland. Cleveland was more of a rough, grimy and thirsty looking city, whereas Miami was a clean more modern tropical beach city.

Being in Miami a person felt rich, whereas living in Cleveland was more of a blue collar city. As Montana sat there enjoying being away from

Cleveland, he thought about how life was gonna be a lot different now that he found a connect.

As he was sitting at the table, Miami showed him a different flavor than Cleveland. Miami was going at a fast pace with the luxuries and money it had to offer and now that the Miami Heat was about to win their second championship, Miami was really going.

There were people from all over the country enjoying the Miami Heat's love. Montana was still salty Lebron left the Cleveland Cavs, but muthafuckas were going crazy over *Lebron James.* There were a lot people walking past Montana's table with Miami Heat's jerseys on. He sat there drinking his drinks living the life, balling.

*Ring Ring Ring* ... Montana's phone went off. He told everybody sitting at the table, "excuse me."

"Hello?" Montana answered.

*"Hey Babe,"* Carmen said as she asked him where he was at. She told him that she had just bought him some clothes to wear. Montana didn't mind Carmen buying him clothes 'cause he knew Carmen knew the type of clothes he wore and when she told him she bought some *Polo* and *True Religion* outfits he knew she had got exactly what he wanted.

Montana told Carmen that everything was good and after they partied that night they were flying back to the city the next morning.

Carmen said, *"okay we're on our way where y'all at."*

"We'll have some drinks for y'all, see if Kim can get us some bud from down here while y'all out and about okay," Montana said.

*"I'm already ahead of you,"* Carmen said as she asked, *"you smell that?"*

Blowing smoke out, *"I got two different flavors of Kush, grape and strawberry. There Kush fly for real."* Carmen continued hitting the blunt a few more times before passing it back to Kim.

*"Poochie said tell her man that she got a nice bikini, she's about to come to the beach in,"* Carmen told Montana relaying the message for Poochie. Montana told Mack what Poochie said.

The drinks started to catch up to Tone as he yelled out in a slurred tone, "tell my sister it's going!" He repeated it to Montana while grabbing the arm of one of the chics sitting at the table, pulling her to him saying, "let's dance boo!"

She declined and snatched her arm out of his grip saying, "I only dance at night. You can come and see me dance at the club if you want to!" She finished her drink and walked back towards the beach with the cheeks of her ass hanging out the side of her bikini bottom.

"Aye what club you dance at?" Tone asked as he watched her keep walking. She looked back and said, "I'm at Club Rosay tonight. Come check your girl out!" She continued walking while making her ass bounce.

"That's what's up!" Tone said.

About the time it took Carmen, Poochie and Kim to get to the beach bar, Montana, Mack and Tone were nice and tipsy. Montana knew he was on a business trip. He still let Mack and Tone do what they do. He told himself that once he got everything in order he was gonna let his balls hang in Miami.

When Carmen and the girls got to the beach bar, Montana was happy to hear that Juan and Jose had their drivers already making their way to the city. By the time they got off the plane the next day, the drivers would be there with five kilos of some top of the line cocaine straight from Peru.

Montana wasn't surprised to see Carmen, Poochie and Kim in their thong bikini sets on with their Brazilian bikini waxes. Carmen let her hair down and her nails were done with her jewelry shining. She walked over and sat in Montana's lap and poured her some Moet.

Montana had the waiter bring more drinks. Mack grabbed Poochie into his arms and kissed her.

Tone was feeling himself so he shot a shot at Kim saying, "I came to Miami and I want some Miami pussy." Kim being on her own turf told Tone that she would turn him on to one of her friends later on that night. Tone tried to holler at every lady that walked past.

Montana was ready to go back to the hotel so he could change and smoke some of that Kush. He hadn't smoked any bud in a minute and without it Montana wasn't feeling himself.

After finishing the last bottle of Moet, they all went back to the hotel to Montana's suite. When they got inside, Mack told them that him and Poochie were going to get dressed and that he wanted some of that Kush they had. Carmen split the Kush up. Kim told Mack that she was going with them. Mack said she could, thinking of that day they made out and Poochie left.

Tone jumped up with an upset look on his face, "damn I just came home and I haven't fucked nothing yet! That's how y'all gonna do me!" Tone said in an upset tone.

Mack spoke up saying, "naw my nigga, it ain't like that lil' daddy, you can roll with us." Mack said with a big smile on his face. Tone's drunk feeling had him fucked up, but he knew what he wanted.

He got up and grabbed Kim's hand saying, "I'm gonna tear this pussy up!" He grabbed his dick with his other hand asking Kim to feel it.

Montana let them out the suite and cut the music on. He rolled up a blunt and he listened to the music and puffed on the Kush. He asked Carmen what she thought about the situation they were dealing with and Carmen said she liked being in Miami and one day when she got her paper all the way up, she would like to open a salon in Miami.

"Babe I'm talking about with what we're doing," Montana said.

"Oh baby I meant to ask you did you know Kim and Poochie was doing coke?" Carmen asked.

"Straight up!" Montana said.

"Yeah I seen them snorting in the room when we were getting our bikini waxes done," Carmen said as she grabbed the blunt from Montana and hit it a few times.

"Kim asked me if I wanted some coke when we was about to get the Kush, but you know me I'm not on that. Kim and Poochie did their thang.

I didn't say nothing, but you know like I know you can't get high off your own supply," Carmen said as she walked in the bathroom to change her clothes.

Montana thought about the situation. Montana knew Mack tasted coke when he copped his dope, but now this situation pops up. Montana got to wondering how much coke did Mack really do. He pulled the *True Religion* outfit out the bag and laid it on the bed.

He called Carmen from the bathroom. She came from the bathroom dripping wet with a towel wrapped around her body. He got to kissing her slightly wet body. He removed her towel revealing her nakedness. Her titties was erected and the wax had her pussy trimmed. Montana licked her titties and worked his way down to her pussy. He licked its inside as Carmen moaned and told him how much she loved him. She turned around and began to give him head. Montana got up and carried her to the patio and bent her over the railing. He looked out at the ocean seeing the sunset. He entered Carmen's pussy from the back with long strokes, while kissing her neck and whispering in her ear. Carmen was loving the view and the feeling Montana was breaking her off with.

She backed off the rail and bent over to touch her toes. Montana smacked and pounded her ass making her cheeks bounce to the sound of the music. He came inside of her and she got up and hugged him. He walked her to the front room, grabbed the blunt and began smoking it before they got in the shower together and got dressed.

Montana asked Carmen what she wanted to do because he wanted to go to a strip club. Carmen told Montana that she was on whatever he wanted to do, but she wanted to see what Tone and them was doing.

She got dressed and picked up the phone and called Tone's new phone and he didn't pick up.

She had Montana call Mack's phone and when he answered Montana said, "what's up my nigga!"

*"Aw man nothing, I'm sitting here making it do what it do. Poochie and Kim over here getting all the way loose with it,"* Mack said.

"Where Tone at?" Montana asked.

*"He right there laying in between Kim's legs,"* Mack said laughing.

"Well we about to fall through," Montana told him.

*"Bring the rest of that Kush with y'all. I wish we could take some back with us,"* Mack said.

"Anything is possible," Montana said as he told Mack they were on their way to their suite.

When Montana and Carmen got to Mack's suite it sounded like they were having a party. There was loud music playing and a loud odor from the Kush was in the hallway coming through the door.

When Mack opened the door Montana and Carmen walked in the suite to the trail of Poochie's, Kim's and Tone's clothes. The Kush lingered in the air. Poochie was in the bedroom getting dressed. She put on a short skirt with a red shirt and a pair of red pumps. Her hair was done in a wrap and she looked herself up and down in the mirror as she noticed that she was losing weight. Her little morning workouts could be the reason that she was toning up. Even though she had been mixing it up with the coke lately. She didn't think she had a drug problem.

Tone and Kim came out the bathroom wrapped together in a large towel booty butt naked. They were caught off guard as Tone pulled the towel accidentally making the towel fall off Kim revealing her naked body. She broke out running back toward the bathroom.

Poochie brought her some clothes. While Kim was getting dressed, Poochie walked in the front room and she was looking good.

Montana double looked at her saying, "damn Poochie I see you looking good." Everybody looked at her. She blushed and asked Montana where the Kush was at. Carmen looked at her and passed her the blunt as she also gave her a hard stare. She noticed Poochie wasn't wearing any panties.

Tone got dressed and came out the bedroom with a smile on his face as if he hit the million-dollar lottery. He was still a little drunk as he came and grabbed the blunt from Poochie and gave his sister a hug saying, "it's going down here. I'm glad I'm home. I'm about to turn it up sis watch me. I got to get me a spot down here 'cause it's going for sure!" Tone said.

Kim walked in the room still feeling a little embarrassed.

"Excuse me everybody," Kim said as she hit the blunt a few times.

"Aye, y'all want to go to Club Rosay, it's the shit down her. Y'all can see how muthafuckas make it rain for real there!" Kim said, "I had went about two weeks ago and they had Rick Ross, Trina and some niggas out of New York there. They were showing out with money. It was said that all twenty something dancers made over a thousand dollars apiece. Though I'm cool on the money. I be wanting to get back to the money," Kim continued laughing.

"With all that ass you got I'll throw some money right now," Mack said smiling.

"Boy go ahead on 'cause Poochie just had you in here saying her name!" Kim shot back.

"I want to stay down here and ball out for the weekend for Tone's release, but we got to get back to the city," Montana said as he looked and noticed the cocaine residue on the coffee table smeared on a mirror. Without saying anything he told himself that he was gonna have a talk with Mack.

# Chapter Seventeen

## *Lil' Shorty*

Lil' Shorty stood at the top of Case Court waiting on CB to come through. CB had spent nearly eight stacks with Lil' Shorty within the past few days. Lil' Shorty started looking forward to seeing him, but instead of CB hitting the corner Shorty saw Dee-Dee crossing the street.

Dee-Dee was the nigga back in the day when it came to fighting. Though he never went pro or won a belt in the boxing ring, he had a helluva name in the hood for knocking niggas out cold. Almost everybody in the neighborhood ducked him or stayed out of his way. He would pull up on dice games and start arguments with muthafuckas that would be winning just to have a reason to knock them out and take their money.

There was a time a guy sold him an ounce of weed and it was a gram short. Dee-Dee knocked the dude out and robbed him and the dude had a pistol on him. Lil' Shorty stood alert when he walked up. He wanted to spend some money for some dope.

Lil' Shorty had heard Dee-Dee had started smoking crack. First he tried to be cool by saying, "Shorty bolt me up for this $40. I would've bought a whole ounce if I knew you was over here putting it down like this!"

Lil' Shorty busted out laughing at the lie he just heard. Dee-Dee instantly got mad asking, "Lil' Shorty what the fuck you laughing at? Nigga I didn't say shit funny!"

Lil' Shorty looked at him like a crack fiend saying, "nigga you ain't got no ounce money. Nigga you smoking!" Lil' Shorty was still laughing.

"Oh yeah!" Dee-Dee said rushing Lil' Shorty with two punches missing the first punch and barely connecting the second one. Lil' Shorty stepped back and upped his hammer letting two shots go at Dee-Dee, hitting him in the leg and stomach.

Lil' Shorty aimed at his head when Dee-Dee fell to the ground. CB came around the corner and yelled, "no Shorty!" Lil' Shorty looked up and caught himself as he hit Dee-Dee upside his head with the pistol then kicking him in the face a few times.

"Bitch nigga you got me fucked up I should kill your bitch ass!" Lil' Shorty said angrily.

CB grabbed his arm and said, "it ain't worth it homie stay getting paper!"

"I fuck niggas up for real!" Lil' Shorty said, "this nigga got me fucked up!" Lil' Shorty continued as another dude led him down Case Court. A crowd was growing at the scene by the time they got to Lil' Shorty's apartment building. Case Court was crowded with people. You heard the sound of the ambulance sirens as they got closer.

They went into Lil' Shorty's apartment. CB asked Lil' Shorty what happened. Lil' Shorty walked in his bedroom and came back out with a lit blunt saying, "that bitch ass nigga got mad 'cause I said he didn't have ounce fare and he smoking crack. He tried to rush me with two punches, so I side stepped his shit and blazed his big head ass with a couple shots to the body, until you showed up in my business!" Lil' Shorty continued bragging.

"I saved your ass nigga!" CB said and continued, "let me buy the rest of that dope you got."

"How you save me? I was about to plug that nigga until you stopped me!" Lil' Shorty said.

"That's what I'm saying! I stopped you from catching a murder beef!" CB said.

"Well since you say it like that! I got five thousand worth of rocks. I can sale you that for four thousand dollars!" Lil' Shorty said, "this right here is the last of it until my people get back with me." Lil' Shorty continued while handing CB the bag of crack. CB grabbed the bag and looked at the rocks he was buying.

"Shorty make sure you holla at me when you get straight my nigga!" CB said as he pulled some money out the bag he had in his draws, counting out four stacks.

"Oh you know I got you for sure. I'm fucking with you my nigga," Lil' shorty said as he heard someone banging hard on his door. Instantly panicking Lil' Shorty put his finger to his lips, with a be quiet jester. He crept to the door to look through the peephole. Thinking it was the police he saw Boo's face instead. Seeing Boo's face made him relax and he opened the door.

"Boo what up?" Lil' Shorty asked as he opened the door letting Boo in.

"Man what the hell you done did out there! Are you cool?" Boo asked.

"Yeah my nigga! I'm straight! I had to chin check the old nigga Dee-Dee!" Lil' Shorty said.

"For what? What the nigga do?" Boo asked looking for a good reason to follow up the beef Shorty was put in.

"He just thought shit was sweet, but he like any other nigga playing crazy can get what they're looking for, you feel me!" Lil' Shorty said.

"I know that's right my nigga, but anyway what's up with that one way?" Boo asked going in his pocket giving Lil' Shorty the money that he owed him and recounting the extras.

"I just gave CB what I had left, but I'll be good in a few hours," Lil' Shorty said as he picked up his phone and called Montana. After it rang a few times he answered.

*"Hello?"* Montana answered.

"What's good unc?" Lil' Shorty asked.

*"Aw it ain't nothing. I'm just sitting here with a little jet lag. I just came back from the sunshine state baby boy,"* Montana said.

"Oh yeah unc. Why didn't you let me know? I would've wanted to go," Lil' Shorty said.

*"That's why right there. I had something to take care of myself. Next time I go I'll let you know because I'm going to kick it. I'll holla back at you in a hour,"* Montana said.

"That's what's up because I was just thinking about you," Lil' Shorty said.

*"I'll get back with you in that hour,"* Montana said again.

"I got to tell you a few things that happened while you were gone, "Lil' shorty said.

*"What's up?"* Montana asked.

"I'll tell you later unc. I'm about to go get me some Kush and I'll be right back here waiting for you in a hour," Lil' Shorty said. He hung up and asked Boo if he could go and get some Kush for him and see what was going on, on Case Court.

Boo walked out the apartment and headed down Case Court. Lil' Shorty went in his room and went in his secret spot and grabbed his bag full of money. He emptied the bag separating the bills and counting it up. Lil' Shorty counted up $24.000.

*Damn,* he thought to himself as he heard someone knocking on the door.

"It's me!" Boo said. Lil' Shorty opened the door letting Boo and Black Dee in.

"What's good Shorty?" Black Dee asked.

"What's up?" Lil' Shorty responded.

"I see you handling your business huh," Black Dee said.

"Yeah man, it's lightweight sweet when you got good shit that's fat," Lil' Shorty continued.

"How can you lose?" Black Dee said.

"Well I'm out right now, but I'll be good in a couple of hours," Lil' Shorty said grabbing the Kush from Boo rolling up a blunt and lighting it up.

Black Dee asked Lil' Shorty what happened out there. Lil' Shorty played dumb saying, "I don't know what you talking about."

"Man the police and Folley out there asking questions about who shot Dee-Dee. The word is that he hurt bad and might be in critical condition. They don't know who done it, but they saying anyone with information leading to a arrest will receive a $5,000 reward. I don't think anybody is going to say anything, but with these broke ass muthafuckas anything is bound to happen," Black Dee said.

"I know that's right," Lil' Shorty said, "aye let me get back with y'all later," he continued. Boo and Black Dee walked out the apartment.

"I'll have something nice for y'all then," Lil' Shorty said as he closed the door behind them puffing on the blunt a few more times. He picked up his phone and called one of his aunts in Washington, DC.

*"Hello?"* Michelle answered her phone.

"Hey there auntie," Lil' Shorty said.

*"Boy what you then done?"* Michelle asked knowing her nephew.

"Dang auntie, why I can't call you. I haven't heard from you in a lil' while and I miss you," Lil' Shorty said half laughing.

*"I know you like I know myself,"* Michelle responded.

"Well, I'm just letting you know that I might have to come out there. I had a little run-in down here, so I might have to come out there for a minute," Lil' Shorty said.

*"Well you better bring some money 'cause I don't got no food,"* Michelle responded to Lil' Shorty.

After giving it some thought about going to Washington, DC, Lil' Shorty started setting his move up. He told himself that he would put Boo in control of his work and have Black Dee on the side in case something pops off or start slowing up, he would be there to help him move the work. He was still smoking and contemplating his moves.

Lil' Shorty went in his room and laid on his bed. He thought about the situation at hand, concerning the shooting. Lil' Shorty didn't care about Dee-Dee getting hurt because he had to be dealt with. Knowing this Lil' Shorty continued to think to himself. *It is what it is.*

He knew he had to go under the radar for at least a week or two. He thought the plans he would put down and what he would tell Montana. As he laid there his phone went off.

"Hello?" Lil' Shorty said as Montana responded, *"open the door, I'm outside."*

"I got you unc," Lil' Shorty said as he headed towards the door to let Montana in. Montana came in the apartment with something stuffed in his pants and laid it on the table.

"Man what the fuck happened out there?" Montana asked.

"Man the nigga Dee-Dee pulled down on me earlier and I let him know off top I wasn't going for no bullying shit and he didn't like what I said, so the nigga tried to take off on me!" Lil' Shorty told Montana.

"Straight up!" Montana replied.

"Yeah man, but you know I slipped that shit and let him have a couple shots to the body. Then I hit that nigga upside the head with my pistol and kicked him in the face a couple times before CB stopped me from shooting that nigga in the head," Lil' Shorty said.

"I'm glad you didn't do no stupid shit like that, shit would really be hot!" Montana said as he opened the bag up and pulled the coke out and laid it on the table.

"What you gonna do now? 'Cause you know police is gonna be at niggas until they find something out?" Montana asked.

"I know that, but I can't miss out on this chance to come up like this. I'm going to DC for a week or two until shit calms down. I thought about everything. I was gonna let Boo and Black Dee run my shit until I come back," he told Montana while looking at the pink looking cocaine sitting on the table.

"Unc what's that right there?" he asked Montana.

"Oh that's Miami (Peru) flake," Montana responded.

"Straight up!" Lil' Shorty said.

"Yeah man you can put at least a half on that right there. Are you sure you want to let them be in control of that?" Montana asked.

"Yeah unc I got it for sure, everything I owe," Lil' Shorty said walking to his room and grabbing the bag full of money.

"Here you go unc, that's 24 stacks right there," Lil' Shorty said.

"Damn nigga, I see you're doing your thang!" Montana said happy about the decision he made to mess with Lil' Shorty.

"Yeah unc, I told you I'm trying to get this paper even in my situation. That 16 yours and eight stacks mine!" Lil' Shorty said.

"What I owe you for this one? Minus this eight stacks?" Lil' Shorty asked.

"Give me $17,000 more my nigga. Come up but be careful!" Montana advised him.

"Oh I told you I been banging these niggas straight $25 rocks. I'm about to put that shit together," Lil' Shorty said as he picked up his phone to call Boo, Black Dee and CB.

"If that's that raw coke I'm about to let go of 27 ounces right now for a stack a piece and make ten bands. I got to go lay low out in DC," Lil' Shorty said.

"That shit crazy!" Montana said.

"I know unc, but if I had to do it all again I would straight up. Aye unc if you want the money now, give me about 20 minutes. My niggas ready to go right now, especially with this work we got right here!" Lil' Shorty said.

"Yeah, I don't mind waiting. Call your people!" Montana responded. Lil' Shorty made his call.

*"Hello!"* CB said, *"what's good?"*

"Bring $27,000 through," Lil' Shorty told him.

*"Straight up,"* CB said.

"That's my word," Lil' Shorty said hanging up the phone.

Black Dee caught up with CB as he seen him going towards Lil' Shorty's apartment building.

"Where Boo at?" CB asked.

"He walked towards Longwood to see if he could talk to Dee-Dee people. You know Dee-Dee a brick nigga, so if he don't take this deal then him or his people can't be down here. I can't play like that," Black Dee said.

"Damn we spoke that nigga right up because there he go right there," CB said as Boo walked up.

"What did they say?" Black Dee asked.

"His people said they'll take $2,500 when they get him together, but right now Folley at whoever done it neck!" Boo said.

"Let's see what Lil' Shorty say," CB said. When they entered the apartment building, the whole place smelled like cooked cocaine. Lil' Shorty let them in and led them to the kitchen. Boo told them what he heard.

"I got $2,500 right now if that's what would deaden this shit!" Lil' Shorty said grabbing the bag from CB asking if it was 27 stacks.

"Yeah man!" CB said.

"Look this right here," Lil' Shorty said pointing to the pinkish looking coke, "is Miami Heat." He was extra hyping the coke up.

"Y'all can make a lot of extras off of it 'cause this A1. I got to leave town for a week or two, so y'all go have the best shit out to put it down like I do. Muthafuckas are going to come from everywhere. Y'all take y'all time and stay low key and get money," Lil' Shorty said handing CB his dope. CB knew what it was and he knew the 27 ounces that he got was a blessing to come up with. He tucked his stuff and walked out the door saying, "I'll be back at y'all soon."

Lil' Shorty was in the process of putting some packages together for Boo and Black Dee when his phone rang.

"Hello?" Lil Shorty answered.

A female said, *"what's up lil pimp baby."*

"Hey there sexy! What's good?" Lil' Shorty asked.

*"You calling the shots,"* Peaches responded.

"I was just wondering what you've been up to since I haven't seen you in about a week," Lil' Shorty said.

*"Well, I took a lil trip,"* Peaches replied.

"I'm about to go on a lil' trip and I want you to go with me."

*"I just came back, but if you want me to go with you I'll go."*

Lil' Shorty told her that he would be to get her in a couple of hours and to be ready. She said okay and went to get ready.

"Who is that?" Montana asked.

"That's my lil' bopper, that's gonna give me head all the way to DC!" Lil' Shorty said laughing.

"That's what's up," Montana said grabbing the money and walking out the apartment to his car.

Lil' Shorty finished packing the packages up. He told Boo what he wanted done with the package and how to get in contact with him.

He gave Black Dee an ounce and told him to bring back $700. Black Dee got his package and left.

Lil' Shorty told Boo again, "look my nigga, I'm trusting you. Here's the keys to the spot. Don't bring nobody over here while I'm gone. Don't make the spot hot and stack the paper up. We got the raw cocaine and if I didn't have to leave I would kill the city with my rocks."

Boo stood and said, "I got you lil' bruh. I'm going to hold you down as if it was my own. Now that you have finally gave me a chance to come up. That's my word I got you."

Lil' Shorty put half along with five stacks and brought Boo 13 ounces broke down in $25 rocks.

"This is 30 stacks worth I'm trusting you with. Let's come up!" Lil' Shorty said to Boo as he washed his hands and grabbed the blunt and picking up his phone. Shorty asked Peaches if she was ready to go and her response was, *"I was born ready."*

"I feel that!" Lil' Shorty responded. He told her to make sure she brought the outfit she wore when she danced at Len Rocks.

*"Why would I wear that when I got something better for you,"* she told him.

"Well bring something 'cause I got something for you for sure," Lil' Shorty said.

*"I know that's right. I been looking forward to seeing you anyway,"* Peaches said blushing.

"I'll be there in ten minutes," Lil' Shorty said to Peaches as he began to get ready to leave town.

# Chapter Eighteen

## *Old Man James and Candy Gurl*

"Hurry up!" Candy Gurl told one of the two young dope boys she was in the hallway turning a trick with.

"Shit! I gave you a twenty. I got to get all of mines!" TJ said as he humped Candy Gurl standing up from the back.

"I'm not going to be out here all day," Old Man James said knowing how long it takes to turn a trick. He had been outside since that morning without a hit of crack. Old Man James was about to smoke earlier when him and Candy Gurl put the money they had together with Dee-Dee's. Dee-Dee told them that everybody that sell dope give him double the worth of dope for his money.

When they saw Lil' Shorty walking towards Longwood, they gave him the money and watched him pull tight on Lil' Shorty. Not knowing what was said, they sat there and watched what happened between Dee-Dee and Lil' Shorty, which was ugly for Dee-Dee and their money.

Old Man James snapped out of his thought when TJ walked out the hallway saying, "nigga you sleep out here, you ain't watching shit!" TJ said.

"Nigga you ain't gave me shit to watch for you either!" Old Man James snapping back. Lil' Moe and Candy Gurl came out the hallway with Candy Gurl fixing her tight ass, dusty blue jeans.

She asked Old Man James, "did you see anybody?"

"I saw CB then I saw Black Dee leave like he was moving."

"Straight up?" Candy Gurl asked.

"Let's go down that way and see if we see Boo," Candy Gurl said handing Old Man James the money.

"Shit what the fuck you in a hurry for!" Old Man James said.

"I ain't had shit to smoke all day and I know Boo got some work, if you say you seen Lil' Shorty leaving in a hurry," Candy Girl said.

"If I don't see him I'm going over there where CB be at. He been coming out with them bricks too," Old Man James said walking up Case Court and cutting through the cut where CB was standing serving a line of people.

Old Man James walked up and one man said, "man that dope so good. I had to flip my rent money to get me some more of this."

"How you know?" a lady asked standing behind him.

"Cause I just hit a piece before I got back in this line. Didn't you hear me say I got to flip my rent money to get me some more," the man said. The lady patiently waited to cop her dope.

"CB what it is," Old Man James said.

"I got this Miami Heat going for $25 apiece," CB said.

"Aw man, come on with that $25 shit Lil' Shorty started, I got 20!" Old Man James said trying to play CB for a fool and keeping the $5 for himself.

"Nigga get the fuck out of here with that bitch ass shit. I set the prices. You know what shit go for down here!" CB said.

"I'm just trying to save a few dollars," Old Man James said.

"Well go somewhere else with that shit!" CB said as he served the rest of the line and started talking to Tonya fine ass.

Old Man James walked off breaking a piece of the rock off he bought for Candy Gurl and put it in his top pocket.

"Aw hell naw, nigga!" he heard Candy Gurl yell as she watched the whole play, play out.

"What the fuck you talking about?" Old Man James said.

"I see you putting a piece of my rock in your pocket!" she said reaching for his pocket.

"Bitch is you crazy!" Old Man James said grabbing her by the throat.

"No … Noo!" Candy Gurl tried to say through his death grip he had on her.

"You my bitch! Everything you got is mine! Hoe!" Old Man James said as he let her neck go and said, "ain't that right?" Hardly being able to breathe she said, "yeah James!"

They turned the corner and walked up Case Court. A few people saw Old Man James and they asked him who was serving. He told the lady with the fifty-dollar bill in her hand that he had something for that.

"Let me see," she said as he handed her the large rock. He got the other pieces of rock out his pocket also handing that to her. She took it and handed Old Man James the fifty and walked off.

"See how I work?" he said to Candy Gurl trying to make up for his actions.

"I see you James," Candy Gurl said.

# Chapter Nineteen

## *Boo*

"Me-Me come here," Boo said as he sat in the living room of their apartment.

"Huh?" Me-Me answered as she walked to the doorway of the living room.

"Help me separate and count this money," he told her.

"Where did you get all this money?" she asked as she walked in to help him count the money.

"Don't ask so many questions. I told you I was about to come up and when I do I'm gonna get you and Ray-Ray out of these projects."

Boo been trying to get enough money to move Me-Me and his little son Ray-Ray out of the projects since Ray-Ray was born a year and half ago. Boo wasn't really a hardcore street hustler and now that he had Ray-Ray his hustle was slow because he wanted to see his son grow up.

He hustled here and there, not really putting himself in harm's way. That was until Me-Me cheated on him. After she had the baby, she told him she wanted more out of life than living in an apartment down in the projects.

Me-Me had met a man who owned a barbershop and bar and lived in his own house. He told her that he wanted her to move in with him, so she could go back to school and get her degree and make something of herself and to also pave the way for Ray-Ray. That's what she wanted to hear. She moved in with him with the best intention of doing what was best for herself and Ray-Ray.

That's when Boo realized that in order to get his family back he had to get on some grown man shit and get his shit together. He started stacking his money up giving it to Me-Me, so she could take care of his son. She realized he had good intentions plus she loved him. She moved back with him hoping that life would get better for them.

They sat there counting the money up. Boo had gathered up all the money from the dudes Lil' Shorty gave work to plus the extras and the total came up to $19,000 and he still had a lot of work left.

Boo told Me-Me to look in the newspaper to see if they had some nice apartments and cars. Though he was just starting to come up and some of the money he had was Lil' Shorty's, Boo still made a lot of money off of the good dope and without his cut from Lil' Shorty. He made $7,000 off of the extras. He knew everybody needed and wanted what he had and he took advantage of it.

Upping the prices almost doubled his profit. The people that was working with them, he sold them a different grade of dope. It was the same dope, but it was cut more. That's how he single handedly outsold the whole strip hustling. He thought of the come up.

Me-Me yelled, "Boo here go one right here!" She handed him the newspaper pointing at the infinity Q45.

"Damn! How much you think I got! You want a good car off top huh?"

"You better believe it. Me and my baby want to be in something safe and reliable," Me-Me said smiling, "what you think."

"Oh yeah y'all gonna always have something nice as long as I got something nice and as long as I got something to do with it. Believe we're gonna be cool," Boo said hugging Me-Me, "let's go get our car. Did you see any apartments?"

"Yeah I seen something I liked but let's do one thing at a time," Me-Me said as they put the money up and walked out the apartment building heading to Boo's car.

*Pop Pop Pop* ... was the sound of the bullets coming from the two door Cutlass as Boo and Me-Me walked out the hallway.

"Ahh!" Boo yelled as bullets struck him in the chest and stomach.

"Get down that's Dee-Dee people!" Boo said as he fell to the ground.

"Boo ... Boooo!" Me-Me screamed, "babe don't do that!" she screamed as Boo's eyes rolled to the back of his head. Me-Me rolled him over and started giving him CPR as she yelled for somebody to help.

"Help! Call 911!" she screamed still pumping on his chest. Two men that saw what happened came to help Me-Me. They picked Boo up asking Me-Me where the car was at. Snapping out of her thoughts she pointed towards her car while pulling the keys out of her pocket. She ran in front hurrying to open the door. They put Boo in the car and headed to the hospital.

CB and Black Dee heard the shots and ran to the strip on Case Court. They were already armed because of the earlier beef. The first people they saw knew to tell them what had happened.

"Who was it? What color car?" they asked as they ran back to the E. 43rd parking lot to get CB's car. They jumped in as CB told Black Dee, "they said that was Dee-Dee people that told Boo they wanted $2,500. They must have wanted to set somebody up if they came back and shot Boo up!"

Boo was driven to the hospital. They saw Me-Me's car parked in the emergency parking spot. CB pulled up and jumped out behind Me-Me's car and ran into the emergency room. Seeing Me-Me's face instantly told the whole story. As they started questioning her back and forth, Me-Me yelled, "what about my Boo dying! What about me, my son and new baby?" Me-Me said crying.

Looking surprised in thought and mad at the same time, CB walked out the hospital leaving Black Dee with Me-Me.

CB called Lil' Shorty's phone.

*"Hello?"* Lil Shorty answered.

"Lil' Shorty!" CB said.

*"Yeah, what's up who this?"* Lil' Shorty asked.

*"CB ... Where you at?"* CB asked.

*"I'm almost to DC, why?"* he responded and asked.

"Man, Dee-Dee people drove by and popped Boo!" CB said.

*"Where he at?* Lil' Shorty asked.

"He ain't make it, he's dead!" CB said.

*"What! Man where Me-Me at?"* Lil Shorty asked.

"Her and Black Dee at the hospital. I left! I'm about to see what's what down there!" CB said.

*"I'm turning around right now!"* Lil' Shorty said making his way back to the Land of the Heartless.

# Chapter Twenty

*Carmen*

Carmen opened up *Ladies First*. She sat in a chair and looked in the mirror. She reflected on her life. She enjoyed the trip they had just came back from, but Carmen had been living life in the streets for the most part of her life and going to Miami and seeing how life was going at such a pace had her looking at her life. She knew she wasn't trying to live life behind bars.

"Hey girl!" Kay-Kay said as she came into the shop. Carmen jumped being shaken out of her thoughts.

"Damn girl you scared the shit out of me! I was thinking about some shit!" Carmen said.

"Are you cool?"

"Yeah I'm okay. How things go while I was gone?" Carmen asked.

"Well you know when a nigga get some power they go crazy. Tara had us detailing the whole shop yesterday, talking about we got to step our game up. She just wanted to make us do something," Kay-Kay said as they started laughing.

"Kay-Kay see if Meech got some Kush. I need me a stick before we start working," Carmen said.

"I know that's right," Kay-Kay said walking out the shop looking for Meech. Bay-Bay, Tara and Gail walked in.

"Hey y'all!" Carmen yelled, "did y'all miss me."

"Hell yeah with Bridzella running the shop, hell yeah!" Bay-Bay said.

"What that mean? Yeah I holded shit down while you was gone and shit went smooth!" Tara said.

Kay-Kay came back in the shop handing Carmen the Kush Meech gave her.

"Thanks y'all for cleaning up and helping keep the shop together," Carmen said giving Tara props all while giving the crew theirs too.

"You welcome," Tara said like the shop was hers.

"Okay … Okay … Okay!" Bay-Bay said irritated with Tara, "you did your job okay!"

"You need to shut up! You always got something to say. Tell them how somebody gonna beat your ass, if they catch you wearing that drag. Tell them that!" Tara said as everybody started laughing.

Kay-Kay butted in saying, "what she talking about Bay Bay?"

"I don't know what she talking about because dudes know me. I ain't on that!" he said.

"You shouldn't have said nothing to me then," Tara said.

"Y'all know that I got the party bus this weekend, so for y'all that still want to go make sure y'all get me the money and let me know how many people coming." Kay-Kay said.

"I want to be one of the strippers," Tara said.

"Don't nobody want to see you Cupcake!" Bay-Bay said busting out laughing.

"If you seen me you'll want me, but you can't so stay down clown!" Tara said making everybody laugh.

"So what are we going to do for this party bus y'all?" Carmen asked walking out the shop to her car with Kay-Kay tight on her heels.

"Girl I wish you could've went to Miami with us. That shit was off the chain down there," Carmen said.

"What happened?" Kay-Kay asked.

"Oh nothing ain't happen, it just go down there. There's always something going down there. It was dudes about 16 years old that pulled up in a Maybach Bentley!" Carmen said as she lit the blunt up, "he gone say I want you baby. Come and stay with me." He told her smiling with a mouth full of gold and diamond teeth.

"Girl, had I been single and younger. I would've ate his young ass up!" Carmen said passing the blunt.

"I feel you, but I'm not going to jail for fucking nobody's kid!" Kay-Kay said.

"Me either!" Carmen said laughing then hitting the blunt again. Tara came up to the car window saying, "aw y'all dirty. Why y'all didn't save me none of that blunt?"

"I didn't know you smoke!" Carmen said laughing off the Kush high.

"Girl stop playing you know I smoke," Tara replied.

"I can't tell you smoke if you don't have none," Carmen said.

"It's cool, I'll buy my own!" Tara said as Meech walked up to the car saying, "Boo got killed on Case Court!"

"What!" Carmen said in disbelief.

"Boo got kilt on Case Court!" Meech repeated.

"Straight up? Don't be lying about no shit like that!" Carmen said, saying a little prayer to herself.

# Chapter Twenty-One

## *Montana*

"Damn Mack!" Montana said as they sat in the kitchen of Montana's house.

"What's up!" Mack replied.

"We're gonna have to take that trip again because that shit is gone already and I haven't been back a whole day. That's four bricks gone."

"Damn that's good shit, but I'm salty my customers got to wait to the next trip. I thought I was getting some of that. I didn't know I was going to have to wait." Mack said with an upset look on his face.

"Man you know I got a ace put up for you. You my nigga, but you can bring all you got on the trip too." Montana grabbed the bag from underneath the cabinet and handed it to Mack.

"You know what you can do with this." Mack opened the bag and pulled the kilo out the bag with a smile on his face.

"This is that raw right here. I'm about to kill em!" The palms of his hands started to sweat and his bowels started to move around in his stomach.

*Ring Ring Ring* ... Montana answered his phone, "hello!"

Lil' Shorty spoke, *"unc! The nigga Dee-Dee's people then killed Boo!"*

"What?"

*"Yeah his girl down in the hospital on 30th right now. Black Dee down there with her. She said they drove by as they were getting in his car and shot him up. I'm on my way back from DC right now!"*

"I'm going down there to see what's going on."

*"Okay unc I'll see you when I get back."*

Montana told Mack what happened as he made several calls.

Lil' Man answered, *"OG what's up?"*

"Aye I need you," Montana answered.

*"What we working with?"*

"These niggas kilt Boo! Come down heavy for me!" Montana said speaking in code.

*"I got you big homie! I'll be down there in 15 minutes. Call me and let me know where I'm going and what I'm doing."*

"Okay let me make a few more calls and I'll get back with you." Montana grabbed an all-black glock .45 caliber pistol with an extra clip from his bedroom safe.

Montana reflected about Boo. He and Lil' Shorty had been best friends since they were little. Montana was their provider and protector and they looked up to him as the big homie. As he sat there hurt, he knew he had to get revenge for Boo's death.

Montana told Mack to drop his work off and meet him down the way. Montana got in his car and headed to the bricks. His phone was ringing off the chain. Everybody that knew him called him to inform him about Boo's situation. The closer he got to the bricks, the angrier he got. He knew Boo didn't have anything to do with the situation. They were now going eye for an eye. Montana knew he had to deaden the situation once and for all and this was the time to represent for his people.

When he pulled up on Case Court CB had the whole crew together waiting on the call. Montana got out the car asking everybody what they knew about Dee-Dee's people. After getting all the information he needed, he told everybody to lay low because it was personal and he was going to handle it.

He and CB went to his car when Mack pulled up.

"Yo Montana, I just came from Longwood and Dee-Dee's people moving right now."

Montana called Lil' Man and told him what was up. They headed to the Woods Apartments. When they pulled up, there were four people loading up a moving truck. One of the guys was sitting on a white car with an AK .47 assault rifle sitting on his lap. Montana picked his phone up to call Lil' Man. He told him to get to the white car. Montana saw Lil' Man and three other people come from around the corner. His phone went dead and the sound of bullets was coming from Lil' Man's AK .47 letting loose.

*Pop Pop Pop Pop Pop* ... They lit the white car up so fast the guy on the car couldn't fire back, but two dudes came out of the apartment bucking back.

*Pop Pop Pop Pop Pop* ... They fired back but that got them AK's pointed at them and that was too much. Bullets caught them from all angles. Three of the four men loading the truck put their hands up.

"I don't have nothing to do with this!" the men said.

A lady helping yelled out, "please don't kill me! I got three kids!" Lil' Man aimed and let two shots hit her in the head. The three men took off running with bullets going right after them, making them fall like bowling pins.

The last guy said, "please don't kill me! I'll tell you whatever you need to know!" He laid there on the ground with bullet holes in his shoulder, back and leg.

"Please!" the man begged for mercy. CB picked him up and put him in the back of Montana's car. They all peeled out towards the eastbound freeway. CB drove while Montana sat in the back seat with dude. He was spilling his guts. He told Montana everything that happened with the thought of living. When Montana thought he knew enough he told CB to pull over and let the man out. The man was hurt, but the thought of getting out the car alive eased his pain away. As he made his way out the car CB jumped out the front seat with the black .45 in hand.

You heard, "noooo ..." He pointed the glock at the man's head letting six shots go, *Pop Pop Pop Pop Pop Pop.*

Montana jumped behind the wheel taking the car to the dump and setting it on fire. He called Carmen and told her to report their car stolen. Carmen knowing shit got handled asked Montana was he okay. He told her yeah then said, "come and pick me up. I'm on Kinsman."

After Carmen picked them up she dropped CB off down the way. Montana and Mack dropped Carmen back off at *Ladies First* and they headed to Montana's safe spot. Montana's phone rang, "hello?"

*"Unc where you at?"* Lil' Shorty asked.

"I'm at the safe spot getting things together. I just pulled up."

*"I just got off the freeway and I'm right here on 30ᵗʰ."*

"I need some of that loud from down there. Be careful because it's hot down there. You know we just lit that muthafucka up, but if you can pick me up a couple twenty sacks."

*"I'll get it and be up there in a minute, I got to drop my friend off."*

He pulled up in front of Peaches' apartment and let her out of the car. He walked around the corner to go get the loud.

---KQP---

Montana went in the back room and opened the safe. He pulled a bag of money out and poured it out onto the table. There were bills everywhere. He had made it back safely from Miami and the profits was lovely. He went through the stacks of money separating the bills. Mack grabbed and separated some of the bills. While they were counting the money, they heard a knock on the window.

"Who is it?" Montana asked through the window.

"Unc it's me!" Lil' Shorty answered. Montana asked Mack to get the door for Lil' Shorty. Lil' Shorty walked in the room giving Montana a hug.

"Damn unc my nigga gone!"

"Yeah he gone."

"You best believe Boo ain't gonna be forgotten. That shit got took care of."

"That's good because you know I got to represent."

"Naw lay low and get your money, it's about your paper!" Montana threw a light punch.

"Ahh! Man you always punching me."

"Yeah that's because you always doing some bull shit. I told you about knocking on my muthafucking window, didn't I?" Montana was still counting the money.

"Where my Kush at?"

"I told you last time if you hit me, I wasn't giving you nothing."

"Man, give me my shit before I kick your ass and help us count some of this money."

"Unc, I would help, but I got to go down the way and get my stuff from Boo's house and make sure Me-Me cool." He walked out the room and headed out the door.

"Call me later."

They finished counting the money and lit a blunt.

"Damn! This a $160, 000 right here. How much do you have?"

"I got 45 stacks put up. After I hit my licks I should have about $60,000." Mack grabbed the blunt and hit it a few times then passed it back,

"Oh yeah, you know Carmen girl Kay-Kay having a set on a party bus to Detroit this weekend." He stacked the money up and put it in his duffle bag.

"I was thinking about going down there to fuck with people's because that trip to Miami is a long ass ride."

"Yeah man it's long, but the trip is worth it." Mack started playing with Montana's pit bulls.

"Damn these dogs then came a long way from being the little puppies they use to be."

"Yeah they have," Montana said, "they on it too. I told you about the niggas that tried to walk Carmen in the house. She told me the dogs was on the niggas asses before they could do anything."

Mack got up and made a phone call. Montana grabbed the duffle bag and put it in his wall safe, then he made a few more calls. After getting everything together, he got the clothes and all the evidence that could link him to the crime and took it outside and burnt it in a garbage barrel. After that he took Mack home and came back home to relax and gather his thoughts.

Carmen called Montana and told him that Tara was about to bring her home.

"I'll see you when you get here Boo. Pick something up to eat before you get here," Montana said as he hung up his phone.

# Chapter Twenty-Two

*Lil' Shorty*

Lil' Shorty pulled up on Case Court in the all-black '96 Impala that he rented before he left for DC. As he rode down the strip he saw a lot of people looking for drugs. With all the shootings that were happening, the police were on high alert in the neighborhood. Trying to hustle knowing how crooked the 3rd District cops were wasn't wise.

Lil' Shorty knew he had to stay out the way due to the incident that happened a few days prior. He looked around to see if he saw CB or somebody from the click so he could see what had been going on. When he got to the middle of Case Court he saw Sue and Moe walking down the street. He pulled up next to them and rolled his window down. Sue being scared not knowing who was in the black car, instantly took cover diving to the ground and rolling over behind a car. Moe looked around to see what was coming.

"Ma! What are you doing?" Lil' Shorty asked. She looked up and saw Lil' Shorty and heard Moe bust out laughing. Sue was embarrassed and mad as hell. She got up and swung her fist at Moe's face with a viscous blow. Moe jumped back still laughing.

"What did I do?" Moe asked.

"You always finding something funny muthafucka! I'm not going to let nobody kill me!" Sue said wiping herself off.

"That's Shorty!" Moe said smiling.

Sue gave Moe an evil look and asked Lil' Shorty, "why the hell are you pulling up like your crazy or something? You know that all this shit is going on and your right in the middle of it. You have people looking for me for the shit you doing!"

She walked to the front of her apartment building with Moe two steps behind her.

"Where are you going?" Sue asked Moe.

"Go open your door and I'll be in there to let you know what's going on," Lil' Shorty said to Sue.

"I know what's going on! And you finding everything funny. Go somewhere else and find that funny!" she said to Moe.

Lil' Shorty got out his car and walked into Sue's apartment to a different look. They had a clean house. Lil' Shorty sat in the front room and asked Sue what she knew about what was going on. She told him that she heard what happened between him and Dee-Dee. Then what happened between Dee-Dee's people and Boo. After that, she told him that the police been asking questions about who's responsible and that there's a reward for whoever has information leading to an arrest.

Lil' Shorty sat back and thought about the situation. Lil' Shorty sent Moe to get some Kush and to see where CB or whoever from the click were at. He knew he had to lay low, but with money he knew he could pull a few strings and get his self out of the situation.

He picked his phone up and called Me-Me.

*"Hello?"* Me-Me answered still upset and crying.

"Me-Me this Shorty. I'm about to come around to your apartment are you okay?" he asked her.

*"I'm hurt but I'm okay!"*

"Open your door, I'm walking around there now." Lil' Shorty put on a dirty hoodie of Moe's to block his face. Lil' Shorty saw Old Man James and Candy Gurl standing on a porch with a few other people. With the hoodie disguise on, no one knew who he was.

Old Man James said, "aye my man, is you looking?" Lil' Shorty kept it moving without saying anything or looking back.

When he got to Me-Me's building he walked in her apartment and Me-Me grabbed him in a hugging position and asked, "what did you do to get my husband killed? He didn't do nothing to nobody!" Me-Me was releasing all the pain and frustration she was feeling.

"I got his son and I'm pregnant. We were just about to go get us a car and a place to live away from these projects! We were looking forward to our future! We had plans on going back to school and opening up a hair salon or a restaurant!"

She was still crying. Lil' Shorty let her get all her emotions out. He comforted her and told her that he would make sure that her and her god kids would be okay.

She excused herself and walked in the bathroom. Lil' Shorty picked his godson up and told him things were gonna be okay.

"Me-Me where that money and stuff Boo got at?" Me-Me came out the bathroom and went into the closet safe and let Lil' Shorty get it. He grabbed the bag that contained the money and the bag of rocks. He opened it up counting everything. There was $28,000 in cash and $16,000 worth of rocks. He split the cash up giving Me-Me half. He told her to open up an account for her and the kids and to get the car and apartment she wanted. Lil' Shorty also ensured her that he would handle everything that needed to be done.

Me-Me thanked him and gave him another hug. She knew that he would be there the best way he could.

---KQP---

Lil' Shorty answered his phone.

*"Where you at?"* CB asked

"I'm over Me-Me spot. What's up?" Lil' Shorty asked.

*"Me, Pimp and Black Dee right here in my back court and we need to holla at you."*

"I'll be over there after I leave here."

He told Me-Me to call him for anything as he was preparing to leave. He packed the bag up and walked towards CB's courtyard. He walked past Old Man James. Old Man James noticed him and started running up alongside of him.

"Lil' Shorty I thought that was you. What's good?" Old Man James said.

"I'm good, I'll be back in motion soon. Wait for me, I already know ain't nobody out here." Lil' Shorty said. He made his way where CB and the rest of the crew was standing waiting for him.

"Look y'all!" Lil' Shorty said, "things are hot out here with everything that's going on, but in the meantime we got to make sure that whoever got away get caught before they get a chance to retaliate like they did with the homie."

"Man fuck them niggas! I swear on everything I'm killing whoever had something to do with it. I love y'all niggas and from today on, I'm going hard on anybody that's not on the team!" Black Dee said.

"That's cool, but we got to get this money and we got to make sure Me-Me, Ray-Ray and the new baby get took care of," Lil' Shorty said handing CB the bag of crack, "put this up or sale it for me."

Lil' Shorty walked back to his car. When he got in and sat there, he pulled out his .40 caliber pistol out from his waistband and put it on his lap. He drove around to Longwood Apartments hoping to see anybody responsible for what happened to Boo. He drove past Dee-Dee's family's apartment and saw that all the windows were shot out and the apartment was burnt to a crisp.

Though he was still mad at the fact, he was happy that the big homie represented for the team. It was on after that.

Lil' Shorty picked up his phone and called Peaches.

*"Hello?"* she answered.

"What's up baby?" Lil' Shorty asked.

*"Hey there lil' pimp."* Peaches was rubbing lotion on her legs and feet.

"What are you doing"

*"I'm sitting her lotioning up after just getting out of the tub. Why? Are you about to come over?"*

"Yeah, I'm on my way over there now." He had been thinking about what she told him when they met. She said when she found out all the details of what she was putting down, she was going to get more money for him.

Lil' Shorty knew she had something up her sleeve, but then wasn't the time for the play to go down. He played it off like he wasn't on it, but in the back of his mind it mattered. He wanted to know what she had going on. He knew she loved his fuck game, so he planned to step it up on her, by going over her house and fucking her for the rest of the night.

Lil' Shorty knocked on her door and to his surprise Peaches came to the door with nothing on but a bra.

"Hey baby!" Peaches said.

# Chapter Twenty-Three

## *Old Man James*

"Hold up Jackie!" Old Man James said. She was about to walk off.

"I'm not about to keep standing over here waiting for somebody to serve me some dope. I just got out of jail, I need me a hit!" Jackie said.

"I told you I just talked to the man and he told me to wait over here and he'll be here in a minute."

"Well he better hurry up because I got shit to do! I haven't even been home yet. My family then paid my bond!"

"How you got all them 20's if you just got out of jail?" Old Man James asked wanting to know where she got the money from.

"They let me out on a personal bond on that stem case, but my people had already paid my bond, so the bondsman gave me the money to take back."

"Well since you spending that $100, can I get my $10 back you owe me?" Candy Gurl said. She was looking for some money to get started with. Jackie gave her a ten just as Black Dee came around the corner.

Soon as Old Man James saw him he said, "see Jackie, I told you somebody was about to come out here. You ain't believe me did you? I be knowing what I'm talking about." He was happy his self that Black Dee hit that corner.

"Black Dee what we doing?" Old Man James asked.

"Oh you know I got it! I got what all these muthafuckas want! What's up!" Black Dee said.

"What you got? You only got $25 rocks right?" Old Man James let Black Dee know he was working customers.

"She got a dolla, so that's four. Dude want two." Old Man James was running customers.

Black Dee looked up and yelled, "nigga I'm not serving this bitch! This hoe is the police!"

"Black Dee what you talking about?" Jackie asked.

"Bitch you know you got knocked with the nigga Rick from KK shit and didn't go to jail. Get the fuck out of here!"

Jackie knew that was her que to get the fuck out of there. She started walking away. Black Dee picked up a bottle and slung it at her, just missing her head.

"Dirty bitch!"

"Dee my fault!" Old Man James said, He knew he was wrong for bringing her to him.

"My fault! It's always your fault muthafucka! All you thinking about is these muthafucking rocks. You don't know shit! You do one more thing wrong, it's gonna be your fault for sho! Now what the fuck y'all got?"

The customers got away from Old Man James not wanting to get shorted for his mistakes. Black Dee grabbed the money from one of the customers named Foots.

Foots told Dee, "don't give me no short shit for what this dumb ass nigga did. Bolt me up playa you know I fuck with cha and need to be. I'll fuck this nigga up for you!" Foot smiled with no teeth showing. Old Man James was mad.

"Nigga you can't beat yo way out a paper bag, let alone fuck with me. You better cop your piece of dope and go ahead on before I beat your ass and take your shit!" Old Man James looked Foots straight in the eyes. Not wanting to chance his rock, he put his rock in his pocket and told his friend to come on. They took off walking around the corner.

"Nigga you not putting nothing down over here. Your lucky I'm gonna still fuck with your dumb ass. You got this bitch working with them po-po's and getting out of jail free whenever she wanted to!"

"My fault for real, I ain't never gone try to take you down. Your family!" Old Man James was holding $35 in his hand.

"What can I get for this?"

"I'm gonna give you two rocks, but you got to watch the streets for me." Black Dee gave him the rocks.

"I can do that, but I haven't had nothing to smoke, so I'm going to take me a hit then I'm off and running." Old Man James was jumping in the air.

"You know I got Case Court on lock running licks."

"Oh yeah, you had a lot of licks coming from everywhere earlier. You want me to hit the Compound for you?" Old man James knew if he got a lot of sales he'd get more of the A-1 dope.

"Yeah man, go take care of your business and hit the Compound up. Hurry up nd come back down here. Where Candy Gurl at?" Black Dee was looking to get somebody in front of his trap apartment building.

"Huh? You called me? Yeah I'll stand out here until he come back," Candy Gurl said hoping he'd give her one of those fat $25 rocks he had.

Candy Gurl had been smoking crack for the past 25 years. Before she lost the life that she had worked so hard for. She graduated from nursing school and became a registered nurse. By the age of 22, she was married and had one child and was pregnant with her second one. That's when her life changed for the worse. At eight months pregnant, her husband filed for a divorce and moved in with his white girlfriend. That hurt Candy Gurl so bad, she bought a gun and followed him to her house. When she saw them come out, she got out her car firing at them. Though she didn't hit no one, she went to jail and was charged with felonious assault and domestic violence. She plead out to a simple charge of domestic violence.

The felony on her record caused her to lose her job and she lost her children in the divorce. She became so depressed, she went to a friend's house and smoked some crack and from that first time and with all the praying from her family, she couldn't stop smoking crack, prostituting or living the life of a cracked out junkie on the east side of Cleveland.

She had different relationships during her addiction, but it was Old Man James that trapped her heart and made her feel safe. He made her want to get clean and live for her.

---KQP---

Candy Gurl walked down Case Court and into a building with Old Man James. When she walked up the first flight of stairs Peaches called her name, she turned around to see Peaches.

"What's going on stranger?" Peaches asked giving her a hug.

"Where have you been?" Candy Gurl asked her.

"I been in and out of town trying to do the damn thang. What have y'all been up to?"

"Girl you know how this shit go! Somebody got to hold the strip down with all the shit happening down here."

"Y'all got some rocks? I need me a hit. Here James go get something for this 50." Old Man James copped some dope and they started getting high.

# Chapter Twenty-Four

## *Montana*

Montana got up early. He had been going through so much lately. He was mentally tired. He got out of bed and put his clothes on and took his dogs out for a morning run.

He hadn't run in a few with how busy he's been. While he was running clearing his mind, he thought of how he was gonna come up. He knew the connect was going straight, but he had a lot shit going wrong. He thought about the situation with Boo getting killed, leaving his girl and kids. Then the situation with Dee-Dee's people and how the police had a reward out for whoever was responsible for what happened. Carmen also told him that she was tired of the street life and was ready for a change of life.

Lil' Shorty had just come back from out of town and he was going through his problems. He thought he was coming up in the game. He was still making shit hot with the situation he started.

Mack was using cocaine here and there. Ever since the trip, it was going back and forth through his mind about what Carmen said about when she saw Kim and Poochie doing coke and how Mack used the coke Juan had.

There was so much that needed to be tightened up and it was Montana that controlled his own destiny. He wanted the money and now that he had the Miami connect, he was about to cut all his loose ends and step his game all the way up like he had planned.

After finishing up his run, he went back to the house. When he got to the backyard he walked towards the car thinking about the blunt he left that night. Just as he was about to open the door, three men came from behind the car.

"Nigga you know what it is!" One of the men said pointing a black handgun at him. Kilo ran around the car jumping on the first man as Kush jumped on the second one, biting him in the face and chest. By it being dark it took the third gunman a minute to get aim on the dogs. Once he did, he aimed and let some bullets fly hitting Kush in the head two times, instantly killing her. Kilo was still mauling the first guy until he regrouped and let four shots go hitting Kilo in the head with all four shots.

Montana was seeing it as an all or nothing situation. He ducked behind the car and tried to make a run for it, but one of the men was on him shooting six shots at him as the other two men started shooting too. Montana was on high alert and was scared for his life, used the darkness to his advantage. He zig zagged as he ran making it hard for them to get a shot. He ran to the backyard and through a few more yards not looking back. When he did stop, he felt his back and it was wet and it started to sting. His breathing started to get short. He got up and made his way out a backyard. When he ran out a lady jumped and screamed thinking he was a robber.

Montana said, "please help me, I been shot!" He fell to the ground. A man ran out the house with a pistol in his hand. The lady told the man that Montana was shot.

"Give him CPR while I go and call 911!" The woman said to the man.

When the ambulance got to the scene to pick up Montana, there were neighbors outside looking and wanting to know what was going on. Carmen came from around the corner asking the police and emergency team, "is that my husband in that truck?" She was fearing that it was Montana in the truck.

# Chapter Twenty-Five

## *Carmen*

Carmen was scared. She was awakened by the gunshots. She thought they were in her house. She had jumped up to find Montana gone when she heard the first four shots. She knew it had to have something to do with Montana. She peeked out of her back window only to see some shadows.

As she looked, she heard and saw the fire come out of a gun held by the shadow. She jumped to the floor grabbing her gun from underneath the pillow and ran towards the back door.

When she opened the door, she heard the shots coming from several different people standing in the same area. She aimed and fired her 9mm in the direction where the shadows were. Two men ran off only to come back and carry one of the other men to a truck driving off.

She went outside to find Kilo and Kush on the ground dead. She looked around for Montana and ran through a yard, then another one. She heard the sirens getting closer and closer. She saw the police cars and the ambulance when she got to the scene. She asked a lady was it a black guy in the truck.

The lady said, "yeah I think so." That's when Carmen looked in the ambulance and saw Montana hooked up to an IV.

"That's my husband!" Carmen said. One of the officers said they needed her to come to the hospital. Another officer tried to console her.

"Let me ride with my husband!" She climbed into the back of the ambulance heading to the hospital.

Carmen waited for the doctors to tell her what was going on with Montana. Three different police officers and two detectives were asking her questions.

"What's his name? What happened? Who do you think is responsible?" one detective asked.

"I don't know who done what! All I know is my husband is back there fighting for his life and y'all is sitting here talking to me, instead of going and looking for who done this!"

"Do you think this is a retaliation from what's been going on?" Detective Folley said, "we know Montana Jones got something to do with all the street wars. We just don't have nobody to testify against him. Tell him we at the 3$^{rd}$ district need to ask him a few questions when he recover."

The detectives left and the doctors came out and told Carmen that Montana's surgery went well and he'll be okay in a few days. Happy that Montana was okay, she went to the phone area and called Lil' Shorty's phone only to get a voicemail. She called back again and Lil' Shorty picked up and said, *"hello?"*

"Shorty this Carmen, Montana got shot but he's good."

*"What! Where y'all at?"*

"We're at MetroHealth Hospital. I really can't talk on this phone."

*"Well stay right there, I'll be right there!"* Carmen walked to the back room to see Montana laying in the bed.

"Boo are you okay?" Carmen asked him giving him a hug and a kiss.

"Yeah I'm good. Them bitch ass niggas thinking they can get me. Must don't know. They say the good die young. So that must make me young and bad huh?" Montana said laughing.

Carmen told Montana, "the detective say he needs to talk to you." Carmen helped him get up and walked him out the hospital. Lil' Shorty was pulling up and he helped him in the car.

"What's good big homie?" Lil' Shorty asked. He had an AK .47 assault rifle sitting on his lap before he got out the car, "what happened?"

Montana got to running the story of what happened down. Carmen jumped in the story telling them what she did.

"We got to take a vacation for a few days," Montana said.

"That's cool, but I got to come up. I got things going on and my niggas putting in heavy work. I got to get shit right!" He thought about Peaches leaving her apartment and him getting the money.

Lil' Shorty dropped Montana and Carmen off at the Embassy Suites Hotel. Carmen and Montana went inside the hotel. He was still injured. The bullet went straight through his back and came out his shoulder. The splint he had on had nothing to do with what he was feeling.

"Boo!" Montana said as he laid back on a big fluffy pillow, "take this pain away."

His phone started to ring. Carmen answered his phone handing it to him all while still making his pain go away.

*"Hello, what's up?"* Mack asked.

"Yeah man, nigga tried to get at me this morning but you know I got away," Montana said.

*"Oh yeah, I'm on my way my nigga! Where are you at?"*

"I'm cool I'm at the Embassy. I need you to take care of my yard. First, with Kilo and Kush and any shells laying around the yard. When you through, get some Kush and bring Poochie. We're about to take a trip back to Miami. Are you ready?"

*"Yeah man you already know."*

"I'm up!"

*"I can't wait; we're coming up for sho!"*

# Chapter Twenty-Six

## *Lil' Shorty*

Lil' Shorty pulled up on Case Court to see the regular customers standing on a porch. He parked and Old Man James jumped up like he hit the lottery.

"There go my main man right here!" Old Man James said giving Lil' Shorty dap.

"Where's everybody at?" Lil' Shorty asked.

"CB and Pimp by CB spot. Black Dee in the building working with me and Candy Gurl on the clock."

"I need to talk to you."

"About what?" Old Man James stepped around the corner.

"Last night when we was out here, Task Force came through and put everybody on the wall and searched us. For those that had illegal shit on them, they smacked them up and told them that if they didn't have no information about all the drugs and killings they were going to jail."

"What they wanted to know?"

"Who is who and who is responsible for the shit that happened to Dee-Dee people in Longwood. They said that they were giving them that was out there two days to find something out or there won't be another piece of dope getting bought or sold from E. 30th to King Kennedy and the reward went up to $6,500 and a get out of jail free pass."

"Oh yeah!" Lil' Shorty wasn't giving a fuck about them.

"Have they been through here today?"

"Naw they haven't been through here and it's been jumping."

"Well that mean we got to go hard now." He grabbed his phone and started making calls. After making the calls people started to come to cop work. CB, Black Dee and Pimp served people up and down Case Court. Lil' Shorty went to the Compound with Old Man James tailing him with the large package of work on him.

"You know your girl was out here last night. She stayed for a while with me and Candy Gurl."

"Straight up!" Lil' Shorty started putting the pieces together about where and what she did that night.

"Yeah she asked about you and she told us that she been in and out of town lately."

"Oh yeah I got to catch up with her." He was trying to hear what he could about her.

"She got caught with a piece of dope last night too, but I don't know what they said or did to her. I told you they said we better have something for them in two days. I didn't get caught with nothing so fuck them. I'm getting the fuck out of here tomorrow until this shit pass over, because I'm not trying to go to jail, ya feel me?"

"Yeah I feel ya!" Lil' Shorty grabbed the bag of crack from Old Man James and started serving the customers.

As they stood there they saw a few squad cars ride and slow down, but none of them stopped like they normally did, which was a good thing, seeing though all the people that were outside buying dope.

Things were going. Lil' Shorty thought to himself, *damn when it's time to re-up. Shit going to be too sweet. I'm glad I didn't stay in DC. Now I'll be able to move down there since my monies up.*

Lil' Shorty thought about Montana's situation. He was wondering who was trying to get at the big homie.

Lil' Shorty turned around to the sound of tires screeching. Three police cars surrounded Lil' Shorty and the group of customers. Lil' Shorty and a few others tried to make a run for it, but they had police covering every opening making it impossible to escape. One detective grabbed Lil'

Shorty and threw him up against the car and read him his Miranda Rights. Lil' Shorty wasn't tripping because he didn't have any drugs on him.

When he was running he saw Old Man James throw the dope on top of the building. He was confident he wasn't going to jail, but he didn't want them to take the $7,000 he made that he had in his pocket. Detective Folley asked him short questions, while frisking him down and running a background check on him.

"Michael Jones lookee here," the short white detective said, "we got a warrant for your arrest."

"For what?" Lil' Shorty asked.

"Attempted murder and felonious assault," the other detective said, "you'll know more when you get to the city jail."

When Lil' Shorty got to the city jail, him and a few other people waited in their cells for phone calls. When he got to his call, he called Montana's phone only to get the voicemail. He tried Peaches and she didn't answer either.

He called CB and had him get in touch with a bondsman and a lawyer. Lil' Shorty had heard of a lawyer named Paul Manning that got a lot of people he knew off their cases. He told CB to call and have him get the money out of his property and get him out of jail.

Two detectives came and told him they needed to talk him.

"Talk to me! I don't have nothing to say! My lawyer is on his way down here! Talk to him!" Lil' Shorty said.

The detective got closer so only Lil' Shorty could hear him and said, "your going down. We got several people waiting to testify to you shooting James (AKA Dee-Dee) Black and we know you got something to do with all the other shootings that's been going on as well."

"Well, if you got all that, do what you do." The detective walked out and started talking to a fiend called Compound. It was said that Compound used to be thorough back in the day, but as time went by, the game caught up to him. Now he was a smoked out crackhead that would do whatever it took to get a hit of crack or free himself of any trouble he may have gotten in.

When Lil' Shorty was walking back from the phone call, he saw Compound walking back to his cell telling another man that he was about to get out of jail because they had dropped the charges on him.

"That's my third time beating these hoes. No fingerprints no case." Compound said.

"Man you a lucky muthafucka because they just charged me with a felony five for the same thing," the man said.

Lil' Shorty told himself that he had to take care of Compound. The next phone call Lil' Shorty made he tried Peaches again.

The turnkey called his name, "Michael Jones!"

"Yeah what's up?" Lil' Shorty responded.

"You got an attorney visit!"

Lil' Shorty walked out the visiting room as Compound walked past him as a free man.

"Lil' Shorty what they got you for? I'm about to be released, do you need me to do anything for you?" Compound asked.

Lil' Shorty looked at him and said, "hell naw nigga! I don't want you to do shit for me!"

# Chapter Twenty-Seven

## Mack

Mack got in his white-on-white BMW. Though things weren't good as things could've been, things were going okay despite the cocaine he got used to using.

He got to Montana's house and pulled in the backyard. When he got out of his car he saw Kush first laying on the ground dead with bullets in her. He took a few more steps around Montana's black Camry and Kilo was slumped up with holes in him and bullet shells were laying on the ground. He picked up the shells and the dogs and bagged them up.

When he walked around the house looking for anything else, he saw a sweatshirt laying on the ground. He picked it up and looked at it. He noticed it had three bullet holes and blood all on it. He put the sweatshirt under his arm and continued to look for stuff. Once he finished, he walked to his car and put the sweatshirt in his trunk. He picked his phone up and called Poochie.

She answered her phone and Mack told her what happened to Montana and that he wanted them to go to Miami with them. She told him that she would go and told him she was about to get ready.

Poochie was tired but she managed to get her things together. While she was waiting on Mack her phone rang. She let the answering machine pick the call up. It was Lil' Shorty. Knowing she was on her way out of town, she let the machine take the message. She continued getting ready.

*"Hello, this Shorty. I got picked up on some bogus charges and I'm down here in the city jail. Hopefully I'll be out soon, but if not I'm gonna need you to come and see*

*me. I'll try to call you later. Okay take care."* Lil' Shorty said as the phone hung up.

"Hello! Hello!" Poochie said as she picked the phone up only to get a dial tone.

*Damn* she thought to herself. She knew she had to tell Lil' Shorty what the detective said to all of them that was outside that night. She was worried because she never had a case before and she wasn't ready to have one. The detective wrote all her information down and left her a phone number to call. He told her he wanted to know who was responsible for all the shootings and he wanted to know where she got the raw dope she got caught with from.

He told her, "somebody is bringing this dope from either Miami or Peru and out the two it's most likely Miami."

That shook her enough to tell him to give her some time to see what she could do. Poochie knew she had enough feelings to never cross Lil' Shorty, but all at the same time she knew she had to come up with something and soon.

She walked in the bathroom and looked in the mirror. Her eyes were blood shot red from not getting any sleep. She ran some cold water on her face and she put some eye drops in her eyes to clear out the redness. She had been going heavy on smoking.

She knew if she put herself in a position, she could be Lil' Shorty's woman and be in good hands. First, she had to finish setting up the plan she was working on. That day would be the day she had to get on her game.

She walked down the stairs when she heard the door opening and Mack walking in with two bags. He sat one on the table and he put one in the closet.

"Hey baby!" she said giving Mack a kiss. He opened the bag and started counting all the money. It was $68,000. Mack asked her was she ready as he stacked the money back in the bag and called Montana's phone.

"Hello what's good bruh?" Mack asked.

*"Aw ain't nothing to it."* Montana answered.

"I took care of that for you. I'm mad for what happened. I looked at Kush and Kilo. They must have been on somebody's ass because they slugged them up for sho, but I took care of everything. Now I'm over here getting my paper together. I'm about to go around the corner to get the Kush then we'll be on our way."

"Well hurry up the plane will be leaving a few hours."

"Alright!" He gave Poochie the keys to the car and walked around the corner. Poochie grabbed her two bags and walked them to the car. She went back inside and looked in the closet to see what was in the closet. She opened the bag and saw the sweatshirt. She didn't really get it until she pulled the sweatshirt out of the bag and saw the blood and bullet holes in it. She thought to herself, why would Mack be holding it.

She put it back in the closet just as Mack came back in the apartment. He grabbed his bag of money and asked her if she was ready. They walked out the apartment and got into the car, to the sounds of *Lil' Wayne's Duffle Bag Boy.*

"Babe this my shit!" Poochie said as she danced in her seat to the music.

She said to Mack, "when we get to Miami and do what we do, let's go shopping. I want to get icy."

"Bitch you ain't putting no work in to want to get icy!" Mack said, "what you can do is go down there and set something up, so we can make some money to get you some ice." Poochie rolled her eyes. Mack reached back and smacked her in the head.

"Bitch you got to be going crazy!" Mack said giving her a look that said, I dare you to say something. Poochie covered her face up as tears rolled down her face.

"Straighten your face up before we get to this hotel!" Mack pulled up in the hotel parking lot and called Montana's phone.

"Hello Montana, we outside." Mack pulled a bag of powder cocaine out his jacket pocket. He opened it up and sniffed it. He handed it to Poochie so she could get her a blow. Poochie grabbed the bag. She stuffed her nose inside and sniffed some of the white powder cocaine.

The rush she felt was powerful, but it wasn't the rush she was looking for as she thought about what had just happened to her.

Reflecting back made her think about her mother, when she was a young girl and how her little brother's father use to fight their mother and how she would have the marks and bruises on her, but she would always find her way back to him. It was like she was in love or addicted to what he had over her.

She stayed with him and Poochie told herself that no matter how much she loved someone, she vowed to herself that she would never stay in an abusive relationship. Mack slapping her in the head was the first and last time that would happen.

She sat there thinking about being with Lil' Shorty and the plan she had for their future together. When she opened her eyes back up, Mack was taking another sniff of the cocaine. He passed it back to her and asked her what she was thinking about. Poochie not wanting to say what was on her mind, she told him she was thinking of way she could get some money for them.

She grabbed the bag of coke and took another sniff as the feeling rushed to her head and down to her stomach. Though she knew in her mind she was about to end the relationship, she had to make sure she had her plan down and that's what she was doing.

---KQP---

Montana was being helped by Carmen as they walked to the car and got in the back seat.

"Hi y'all!" Carmen said as she gave Poochie a hug and grabbed the weed Mack handed her to roll up. She lit it and passed it to Montana.

"Damn I needed that!" Montana said as he inhaled the smoke and blew smoke circles out.

"Montana are you okay?" Poochie asked as she saw the splint he had on holding his shoulder up.

"Yeah I'm good Poochie. You know I'm a gangsta. I'm not going to let nobody ever catch me slipping again. You feel me!" Montana said passing the blunt to Mack.

# Chapter Twenty-Eight

*Carmen*

Sitting in the hotel with Montana, Carmen picked her phone up and made a few calls. First, she made reservations for them to go to Miami, then she called Tara and asked her to open up the shop for her.

She walked in the bathroom and texted another number and waited. When her phone rang back she answered it on the first ring.

"Hello!" Carmen responded.

The person on the other end answered, *"he doing it now."* She informed Carmen of everything that the person did. She noticed he picked something up and tucked it under his shirt as if he was hiding it.

"Okay," Carmen said, "call me if anything else happens." She came out of the bathroom and started back making love to Montana.

After making love Carmen sat up and asked Montana, "who do you think is responsible? Do you know or have an ideal about any of this?" Montana said he didn't know.

Carmen told him how she felt and how much she loved him. They started going back and forth telling each other about what happened and who and how they thought things could have happened. Even though Carmen didn't reveal her true thoughts, she felt like she had an idea. Her mind was going crazy thinking about what could have happened. She knew she had to do something and with God willing she would do everything in her power to find out what was going on. She thought of a way to see if her thoughts were right.

Montana's phone rang. Mack told him that he and Poochie were outside waiting for them. Carmen grabbed their stuff and helped Montana outside to the car. They headed to Hopkins Airport to catch their flight to Miami.

---KQP---

When they arrived to Miami it was different from last time. It was replaced with clouds, rain and thunder. Miami International Airport was still crowded. People were still going on about their way like the sun was shining bright.

Carmen called Kim and told her that they had just touched down and they were waiting for their cars to be dropped off. She also told her that she wanted to have a ladies' night out with her and Poochie.

Kim asked where Poochie was at. Carmen handed Poochie the phone saying, "Kim wants you." Poochie grabbed the phone, "hello," Poochie said.

*"Hey girlfriend! How have you been doing?"* Kim said.

"I been doing good. What's up with you? How have you been?" Poochie responded.

*"I been good. I can't wait to see you."* Kim said reflecting on the last they were together, *"I started to send for you. I missed you so much."*

"Girl your crazy. You should've sent for me, I would've came." Poochie thought about getting closer to the connect through Kim.

"Well hopefully you don't just think about it and you do it," Poochie continued as she laughed.

Mack said, "tell Kim I said what's up. Tell everybody I said what's up and make sure they're ready to kick it tonight."

"Okay we're about to go to the hotel. Once we get settled in we'll see you when y'all get here," Poochie said as they got in the Cadillac they rented and headed towards the Marriot hotel.

Once they were there Carmen went through her luggage and grabbed a camera and took some pictures of the room and off the balcony of the view of downtown Miami. The rain made the day dark and cloudy and it was only 3:15pm. Montana asked Carmen if she knew where they got those different flavors of Kush from. Carmen and Poochie said yeah at the same time. Carmen told Montana that her and Poochie would go get some.

They got up and walked out the room to the car. When they got in the car Carmen asked Poochie was she okay. Poochie said yeah, but she wasn't okay. She broke down and started crying, shaking her head. Carmen consoled her and asked her what was wrong. Poochie feeling Carmen's love came out and said she wasn't happy with the way her life was going and she felt she needed help with getting herself back together.

She told Carmen she was using more and more drugs and she told her about Mack slapping her and how she wasn't happy with him and how she wanted to get away from all the shit they were doing. She told Carmen she wanted to start a family and career with someone she can love for the rest of her life. She cried on Carmen's shoulder saying how she wish and wanted a life like hers.

Carmen told her that life has ups and downs for everybody that live and what don't kill you, only makes you stronger. They sat there going back and forth about what was going on.

Carmen asked Poochie if she knew anything about what has been going on with Montana. She said no but she thought to herself about the sweatshirt Mack put in her closet with the holes and blood stains on it. Poochie wanted to say something, but she didn't feel the time was right to say what she wanted to say, but she knew in due time she would tell Carmen about the sweatshirt.

Getting herself together Poochie said, "long as I got you, I think things are going to be okay. Now let's go get that Kush and get ready to go and ball out. We're in Miami," Poochie said wiping her face.

Carmen started the Lac up and headed to go get the Kush. The sun cleared most of the clouds and the day was starting to brighten up. They got on the freeway and rolled through downtown Miami towards South Beach. Carmen's phone rang and it was Kim.

*"Where y'all at?"* Kim asked.

"We're going to cop some weed, what's up?" Carmen responded.

*"Nothing I'm just wanting to kick it with y'all."* Kim replied.

Carmen pulled up to the marijuana store. She ran in and got what she wanted and went back out to the car to find Poochie laughing like she was hearing the funniest joke she ever heard.

Carmen told Poochie to tell Kim to meet them back at the hotel. When they got back to the hotel room Montana and Mack were sitting in the living room negotiating with Juan and Jose. Carmen wasn't trying to stop them from negotiating their business, so she and Poochie spoke gave them hugs, and walked to the back bedroom.

Carmen cut the music on. She pulled the Kush out of her purse and rolled two blunts and lit them.

She took one out to Montana and said, "that's blueberry Kush right there."

Juan chimed and said, "what you got for me sis?"

"Oh I ain't know, but it's more where that came from, you want one?" Carmen asked.

"No thanks, I was just playing, but I'll take a drink." Carmen went in the kitchen and got them some drinks and walked back to the back room where Poochie was sitting on the bed fixing her hair.

"What are you doing?" Carmen asked her.

"I got to do something to my nappy head," Poochie responded.

"You know your hair is not nappy. Here let me see," Carmen said grabbing the comb from Poochie and going to work on her hair. It didn't take much considering the texture of Poochie's hair. Soon as Carmen finished and picked her blunt back up the door opened up with Kim walking in.

"Hey y'all!" Kim said as she danced to the music.

"What's up girl!" Carmen spoke.

"Hey there!" Poochie said. Carmen and Poochie both gave Kim hugs.

"Who did your hair?" Kim asked.

"You know Carmen just finished getting me together," Poochie said looking in the mirror.

"Carmen you got me looking fine as hell. I'm ready to go out right now." Poochie was doing her booty dance in the mirror.

"Well if you're trying to stay looking good, you better stop dancing before you mess your hair back up," Carmen told Poochie.

Kim asked, "touch my hair up for me Carmen and let me smoke with you." Carmen sat her down and passed her the blunt. Kim hit the blunt and asked Poochie what she was wearing for the night.

Poochie said, "I don't know what I want to wear. I'll pick something nice out later."

"Okay well we can go shopping together, because I got to get me something to wear too," Kim responded, "what have you been doing?" Kim asked Poochie.

"What you mean?" Poochie replied.

"You lost a lot of weight since the last time I seen you," Kim said noticing Poochie.

"For real!" Poochie said turning around looking at her booty in the mirror, "have I lost a lot?" Carmen knowing what it was helped Poochie out and said, "you lost weight but it look good."

"You just knocked your extras off," Kim said agreeing with Carmen.

"Where we going tonight? I'm gonna make niggas want to take this pussy tonight!" Poochie said laughing and dancing around freaky.

"Girl you crazy!" Kim said. Carmen finished curling her hair and lit another blunt up. She walked in the front room. Soon as she walked out the room, Kim grabbed Poochie hugging her tight. She kissed her with a lot of tongue, while rubbing her booty in the same motion.

"I missed you a lot baby," Kim said.

"Why you ain't send for me then? I would've came down here and put it on you," Poochie said rubbing her coochie.

"You know how to flaunt that shit girl! Fuck a nigga taking that thang. I'll fuck around and take that cookie," Kim said licking her lips.

"Gone girl, let me get up out of here before you start something you won't be able to finish," Poochie said laughing reeling Kim in hoping she fall right in the middle of her plan.

"Well start something. I know I can handle whatever come at me." Mack walked in the room hearing the last words Kim said.

"Oh yeah, so that mean you can handle all of this," Mack said holding his dick smiling. He grabbed Poochie's booty letting her know Poochie was his and if she wanted her she had to take him too.

"You already know how I get down," Kim said, "after we get back from shopping."

"Shopping!" Mack repeated.

"Yeah shopping, we about to go get something to wear for tonight. You want to come with us?" Kim asked wanting Mack to cover their bill.

"Yeah I'll come with y'all," Poochie thought about the shopping spree she wanted.

# Chapter Twenty-Nine

*Montana*

Montana, Juan and Jose sat in the front room talking as Mack walked to the back. Juan asked him what he wanted to buy. Since he made out good from the last package. Montana told him he wanted to score a few more times. If things went right, they would make out. Jose asked him how much money he had to spend, because he had just got a lot of coke and he was able to serve him for his money and front him for the same price.

Montana knew with the front he would be able to serve all of his regular customers, plus whoever else needed a connection and make enough money to be ready to start falling back from the game.

Montana was going through a lot, considering somebody was trying to rob him, but he knew that was part of the game. He told himself that he had to tighten up on his shit, which meant he had to get a new spot and put some space between everybody he associated himself with.

He told Jose he had $180,000 and Mack had $70,000, but he was going to only be reliable for his front. Juan told him to handle the package his way, meaning serve Mack for his money.

Mack came from out the back room, "I'm going out shopping with Kim and Poochie."

"Okay," Montana said. He told Carmen that he, Juan and Jose was going to take a ride. Carmen knowing Montana was in safe hands said okay.

They left and got in Jose's black BMW truck. Jose was getting money for real. The rims and flashy stuff was nothing to him. He had been there and done that, but he still love being around women. He stopped and pulled up in a parking lot and went inside a local strip club.

Jose asked Montana if he saw anything he liked. Montana said yeah, but he had to run it past Carmen before he did anything. That made Juan respect him more because he saw that loyalty meant something to Montana and that gave Juan a whole new look on Montana.

"Girl! That's Jose right there!" Rumpshaker said to the new girl named Pinky.

"Where?" Pinky asked looking at all three of them sitting at the table.

"The one with the blue *True Religion* jogging suit on," she answered.

'Who is he?" Pinky asked.

"Girl you can't be from Miami if you don't know him and his brother Juan in the white jogging suit," Rumpshaker answered.

"Nope I'm from Cleveland," Pinky replied.

"Well them brothers are like kingpins down here. The word is they're worth millions of dollars and they love black pussy."

"They say Jose bought 15 dancers all new cars before. He didn't even have sex with none of them. He just said today was their lucky day, so when dealing with them be extra nice Boo. You might be the one to make today our lucky day," Rumpshaker said giving Pinky the up on them. Pinky laughed as she walked past their table with an extra hard switch.

"Damn! Who is that?" Jose asked.

"I don't know; I haven't seen her before," Juan responded.

"Damn you can put a drink on her ass for real," Montana chimed in.

"Call her over," Jose said

"Hey baby what's good?" Juan asked.

"Hi y'all! Y'all want a dance?" Pinky asked them flirtingly.

"Hell yeah I want a dance and I want to get to know you. Is that cool with you?" Jose asked.

"I'm at work right now, but my name is Pinky and I'm from Cleveland," Pinky asked.

"Cleveland!" Juan said.

"Yeah that's where I'm from," she responded.

"That's where my man is from," he said pointing at Montana, "do you know him?"

"Not right off, but he look familiar, where is he from?" she asked.

"DTW," Montana spoke up not really wanting her in his business.

"Oh yeah I know a few people from down there. My girl Carmen got *Ladies First* hair salon down there." All three of them looked at each other and bust out laughing.

"What's so funny?" Pinky asked.

"It's just funny that out of everybody in Cleveland you say Carmen's name and funny enough she's down here," Jose said.

"For real? That's my girl. Tell her I'm down here getting to this money." Jose watched as Montana acted as if he was not listening to their conversation about Carmen.

"So what are you doing tonight?" Juan asked.

"I don't have anything special going on tonight, but I am down here trying to get this money," she answered.

"Well come and party with us. We're gonna do the damn thing," Jose said as Montana answered his phone.

*"Hello you have a collect call from Shorty,"* the automated phone system said, *"if you wish to accept the call press one or if you wish ..."* Before it finished Montana pressed one.

*"Hello unc! What's going on!"* Lil' Shorty said.

"Where you at?" Montana asked.

*"I'm in the County Jail. I got picked on attempted murder, felonious assault and some other shit. I called Paul Manning and he working his magic for me. Until then I got to lay low key. Where are you at?"*

"I'm down here in Miami, I just got down here, hold up," Montana told Lil' Shorty, "excuse me y'all let me take this call, I'll be right back," Montana said to Juan and Jose as he walked towards the restroom.

"Hello, now what happen nephew?" Montana inquired.

*"I got picked up on the Compound. They didn't find anything, but the detective said I'm responsible for all the shit that's been going on and he's gonna get me and whoever else he think is responsible. I got $7,000 in my property, hopefully this lawyer get it and get me out,"* Lil' Shorty replied.

"You know I'm gonna take care of it. Let me know what happen." Lil' Shorty's phone line said there was ten seconds remaining.

"Stay up nephew, I'll be back in a few days, get with me." Montana walked back to the table where Juan and Jose was still talking to Pinky

"You through?" Juan asked.

"Yeah man, I had to talk to my people back at home," Montana answered.

"Is everything okay?" Jose asked.

"Yeah shit cool! What's this right here?" Montana asked the both of them about Pinky.

"She's gonna kick it with us tonight," Jose said. Pinky smiled while sitting and grinding on his lap.

"Somebody else wants me to kick it too," she said while still moving around on his lap a little more.

"I know that's right," said Jose.

"Let's go and get ready for tonight." They finished the rest of their drinks. They told Pinky they would see her later and she said okay. She gathered the money that Jose left her and went to the back room smiling. She thought about the money she might make later on that night.

She wondered what Carmen was doing down in Miami with Jose and Juan. *Was she hauling drugs for them or was she still dancing.* Whatever it was, her knowing Carmen she knew it was about some money and if it was she wanted to be a part of it.

Pinky thought about what she wanted to wear. She looked back and saw them all walking out the door.

"Jose I see girly got you open," said Montana.

"Si, I want to dance in them pants," Jose said doing a little salsa dance laughing.

"Yeah she is nice. I might have Carmen get her for me," Montana said.

"You got it good, your woman bad and she let you do what you do. You're a lucky man," Jose said.

"Let's go finish this business and we will go party after we finish," Juan said. Both Jose and Montana agreed.

Montana told them that he wanted to chill before going back to Cleveland, because of the incident he needed to heal up. Juan told him to take all the time he needed. He wanted him to be able to protect himself and being well made his chances better.

The incident of the robbery popped up in Montana's head again. He thought about how everything happened over and over. He never brought no one to his house. He knew it had to be somebody close he knew sent somebody at him. He tried to think of who would try to do some shit like that.

Jose asked, "Montana are you okay? You zoned out on us."

"Yeah I'm good, I just thought of the incident that happened. These niggas tried to get at me. They waited until I came back from running my dogs and tried to jump out the cut on me," Montana responded.

"Straight up!" Jose asked.

"Yeah man!"

"When was this?" Juan asked.

"This morning. I checked out the hospital. I gathered my stuff and came down here," Montana said.

"So your telling me somebody tried to abduct and shoot you this morning?" Juan asked.

"Yeah man, they tried to get me, but my baby came through for me! She was right there busting her gun for me!"

"Straight up?" Juan asked thinking back to the time when Carmen saved his and Jose's life.

They had made a major drug drop at a friend's house. There were strippers dancing and people partying. While they were in the backroom making the exchange, three men came in with their guns. They said y'all know what this is in Spanish. Juan made a move to stop them. One of the gunmen shot him three times, hitting him once in the stomach and twice in the leg. He fell to the ground just as another man brought Carmen and three ladies to the backroom. Carmen hearing the shots went into survival mode. She asked if she could help Juan.

The other ladies were screaming and crying while they were down on the floor. She felt his wound and noticed he had a gun on his waist. She looked back and saw that two of the three men were gathering up all the drugs and money. The other man was tying Jose and two other men up with his back turned to her. She grabbed the gun off Juan's waist and opened fire with the .45 caliber on the three robbers. Hitting all of them several times to the chest and head, making them fall.

The last man turned around with his gun in his hand. He started letting shots go. He grazed Carmen on the side of the head. He and Carmen started exchanging shots at each other. He shot Carmen in the shoulder and she shot him in the face above his right eye, making him go straight out. Jose was able to get himself loose. He made sure the robbers weren't able to do anything. He made a way for them to get away.

Carmen had a shoulder wound, but it wasn't anything that the $200,000 wouldn't have cured. She went and got the first plane smoking back to Cleveland. The true story was yet to be told.

One of Jose partners went down for the murders, that got knocked down to manslaughter charges. He did three years and was released.

---KQP---

*Ring Ring Ring* … Montana's phone rang.

*"Hello, where are you at?"* Carmen asked.

"We just left the bar?" Montana answered, "what's up?"

"I'm about to go shopping and I'll see you when y'all get back to the hotel, okay," Carmen said.

Montana, Juan and Jose drove to a house that looked like a small sized mansion.

"Who stay here?" Montana asked Juan.

"This one of my pieces of property that y'all can stay in while y'all down here. I own a few that I got down here, but this one right here should be enough to hold y'all up and keep y'all out the way, until y'all ready to go back to Cleveland," Juan answered.

"That's love my nigga," Montana responded. Juan handed him some keys and said, "it's a truck and a car out in the garage too."

"That's what's up!" They walked to the back of the house and Jose grabbed a duffle bag out of the trunk of the car and said, "whenever your ready." He opened the duffle bag up and showed him 20 bricks of coke. He closed the bag back up and put it back in the trunk of the car.

"When your ready, I'll have our driver ready for you." He pulled his phone out and dialed a number and told them to come and pick the car up. They walked inside the house and talked about the come up Montana would get and the help that they would give him if he needed it. Montana told them that he could handle it and he would be good once his shoulder healed up.

After going over everything that needed to be done. Montana had them drop him back off at the hotel. When he got there, Carmen had just got back from the mall. She had bought several outfits. Montana told her about the house and cars Juan said they could use.

"Oh yeah, we met this chic name Pinky from Cleveland that said she knows you," Montana told her.

"Oh yeah where was she at?" Carmen asked.

"She was at this strip club we went to earlier. Jose was all on her. She supposed to come out with us tonight," Montana said.

"I can't wait to see her, that's my girl. We used to get money together. How was she doing?" Carmen asked.

"From the looks of that ass, she's fine as hell!" Montana said as they both started laughing.

"I know that's right!" Carmen said continuing to laugh.

# Chapter Thirty

## *Mack, Poochie and Kim*

"Why you don't buy me this one?" Poochie asked pointing to a two-carat diamond ring.

"Girl you tripping you act like we're about to get married or something," Mack answered her.

"We're fucking every day and we're not married," Poochie said in a smart way.

"Girl I told you about your mouth before!" Montana responded.

"You say whatever you want to me, but when I say something to you, it's watch what I say," Poochie said as she walked away and looked at another ring in Jared's jewelry store.

"You damn right bitch! I wear the muthafucking pants around here!" Mack said as he thought about checking Poochie about her attitude. Then wasn't the time, because he was thinking about getting with Kim and Poochie. The last time they were together, he put it down, but Mack knew if he knocked Kim off then the hook would be his.

He looked at Kim and said, "you see this shit I got to go through. I didn't say I wasn't gonna by her the ring. I was just fucking with her, but her attitude she go make me not want to fuck with her," Mack said.

"Well you know like I know. If you want to keep your girl, then you better take care of home, because whatever you don't do, another person will," Kim said as she walked beside Poochie.

"What are you looking at?" Kim asked her.

"Nothing really I'm just looking," Poochie said as Mack walked up behind her and said, "gone and get what you want Poochie, but don't go crazy."

"For real!" Poochie said not believing what Mack said, "boyee don't be playing with me, you know I want to get icy!" Poochie said examining the prices of stuff she wanted.

She tried on several chains and bracelets and was about to try on some more until Mack said, "girl you better hurry up and get something before you don't get nothing." The tone in his voice made Poochie's mind up.

"Excuse me, can I get this necklace right here," Poochie said pointing to an all gold necklace. The price tag was $3,600.

"I see you made your mind up quick," Mack said looking at the price tag.

"Damn you trying to break me huh?" Mack said as Poochie and Kim broke out laughing.

Still laughing, "Kim said let me know if you can't handle it."

"Oh I got it, I'm getting this out of y'all ass tonight, laugh at that!" Mack said as they left the jewelry store, on their way to buy clothes for that night. As they walked through the mall, they stopped at *Ladies Foot Locker* shoe store.

"Let's go in here," Kim said with Poochie right on her heels. They walked to the *Cleveland Cavs* section.

"I'm about to get me something nice to wear," Poochie said grabbing a medium sized *Cleveland Cavs* dress holding it up to her, "this is gonna make me look good tonight."

"Girl anything you wear is gone have your ass looking good, ain't that right Mack?" Kim asked Mack as he stood there in a daze shaking his head.

"Girl you know I'm wearing the same thing, but mine gonna be Dwayne Wade's from Miami Heat," Kim said to Poochie.

Mack replied, "don't start no shit and it won't be none."

"That's what I'm saying," Kim said. Mack walked next door to the *Footlocker* to get him something to wear. He grabbed a *Cleveland Browns* jersey with a matching hat. He thought about how it would look with the jeans he already had.

*Yeah that's gone go,* he said to himself. He looked up and saw three dudes talking to Poochie and Kim. Mack just stood there and watched them. Two of the them were draped in platinum jewelry, with one wearing a *Gucci* outfit. The other one was wearing a *Polo* shirt with some matching *Nike* tennis shoes. The third one that was carrying three bags, was wearing a white t-shirt and jeans. He had so many gold chains on that one would think he was a rapper celebrity.

Mack thought to himself as Poochie looked his way and finished shooting her shot at the third man. Mack gave her the nod as she pulled out her phone to exchange phone numbers. Poochie and Kim finished talking and walked towards *Footlocker*. Poochie asked Mack was he ready.

"Yeah I'm ready. We got to go pick up something to smoke before we head back to the hotel." Poochie asked Mack what did he buy out of *Footlocker* as she looked through his bag. Mack grabbed her and rubbed her booty.

"I see you doing your thang," Mack said to Poochie.

"I told you I got you, as long as you got me," Poochie replied.

"Damn I thought you had me regardless," Mack replied smiling.

"I do!" she said.

Kim chimed in, "y'all ain't about to keep going lovey dovey on me, cut me in or cut it out!"

They left the mall and headed to the hotel.

# Chapter Thirty-One

## *Lil' Shorty*

"Lil' Shorty! What's up?" Lil' Meech yelled.

"Who is that?" Lil' Shorty hollered back not being able to see through the cell bars.

"This young Meech," he answered.

"Oh yeah what's up! What are you back here for?" Lil' Shorty asked.

"Man the police say I got a assault on a police officer. I was out there when you got arrested yesterday. I ran the other way when you took off running. I got caught on the other side. They say when I yanked away the detective lip bust, so I don't know what they are gonna do with me. I hope they just straight release me. What's up with you? Did they say anything to you yet?" Meech asked Lil' Shorty.

"Naw I'm still waiting. My lawyer says he gonna get me off, but you know how that is," Lil' Shorty answered.

"Michael Jones!" the turnkey yelled.

"What's up right here," Lil' Shorty responded.

"Do you want the telephone?" the turnkey asked.

"Yeah I want it!" Lil' Shorty called Peaches number again.

*"Hello,"* Lil' Shorty heard Peaches say.

"You have a collect call …" Peaches knowing it was Lil' Shorty hurried up and pressed one accepting the call.

"Hello Peaches," Lil' Shorty said.

*"Hey baby what's up?"* Peaches responded.

"Where have you been at?"

*"I'm out of town, that's why I haven't been down there, but I need to talk to you. How have you been?"* Peaches asked.

"I'm cool, I'm waiting to get out, but until then I'm sitting here thinking about you," he replied.

*"Baby listen, I thought about a lot of things since I met you and I know you might not believe me, but I want to change for you,"* Peached said.

"What do you mean?" Lil' Shorty asked.

*"I want to be your woman and part of your future,"* Peaches said as Kim asked her who she was talking to, *"Look I can't talk right now, call me some other time,"* Peaches continued as she ended the call.

"I don't know when I'll be able to …" Lil' Shorty said before hearing the dial tone.

*Muthafucka! I can't believe this bitch just hung up on me! What the fuck!* Lil' Shorty thought as he dialed another number calling CB. CB accepted the call after going through the system.

CB answered, *"What's up bruh? I talked to the lawyer, he said he's getting you out, but the prosecutor and detective are trying to not let you out."*

"Why not?" Lil' Shorty asked.

"They think you got something to do with all the shit that happened in Longwood Apartments," CB answered.

"Did you see Old Man James?" Lil' Shorty asked.

*"Yeah I seen him and luckily I did,"* CB answered.

"Why you say that?" Lil' Shorty curiously asked.

*"Because the lil' nigga Q came and got me and told me how the police trapped you up and how Old Man James threw your stuff on the roof and got away. Old Man James went back and climbed on the roof to get your dope, but to his surprise I was coming right around the corner as he was climbing down. I told him to give me your sack and his bitch ass gone say, what are you talking about CB. I sucker punched his ass in the jaw and that's when he remembered what was going on,"* CB said laughing.

"Straight up, he tried that?" Lil' Shorty asked.

*"Yeah man, he gone say, I was about to bring it to you, why are you tripping man. I said why the fuck did you ask me what I was talking about if you already knew then. He said because I want to make sure somebody seen me give it to you, so I wouldn't get blamed for no bullshit. I told him, man hand me that stuff before I smash your ass out. He had the nerve to ask what are you gonna pay me then? I told him you lucky I don't kick your ass for trying to pull a fast one on me. He gone say man CB I need you, he turned around being paranoid and said listen I got to get out of here because Folley came through here and told me that if I didn't have no information for them soon, I'm going to jail and I ain't about to go to jail. Lord knows I'm not. He started crying saying that, you told him that you was gonna make sure you looked out for him. He was talking about how he ran your licks and how you was gonna bolt him up when you were finished. He gone say to me, so I'm looking for you to bolt me up or you gonna have to kick my ass, because he wasn't leaving there without getting bolted up. I hit his ass with a left hook and he fell to the ground, then I put all kinds of whoop ass on him,"* CB said cracking up.

"Straight up?" Lil' Shorty said as he continued listening.

*"Yeah man, but I'm not gone lie I paid the nigga six rocks. After he got up and he came back to his senses. He put the rocks in his mouth and rushed me trying to slam me. I stepped back and hit him with a upper cut, followed by a hook to the head and he took off running,"* CB said still laughing.

"CB you're crazy, I did owe him," Lil' Shorty said.

*"Well he should have waited for you,"* CB said continuing to laugh.

# Chapter Thirty-Two

## *Carmen*

Carmen walked in the hotel and laid the clothes she bought for her and Montana on the couch. She got the Kush out of her purse and rolled it and lit the blunt up. She grabbed her phone and checked her messages.

After she was done checking her messages she walked in the bathroom to run some bathwater. When she came out the bathroom, Mack, Poochie and Kim were walking in the door.

"Hey y'all!" Carmen said happy to see them back from shopping. She was getting ready for the night.

"Look! Look!" Poochie said to Carmen showing her the necklace Mack bought her and the outfits she and Kim bought.

"Girl y'all going crazy," Carmen said looking at the dresses they bought.

"I'm going to party!" Poochie said shaking her ass.

"Girl how short that dress is your panties are going to be showing," Carmen said.

"Come on Carmen, who gonna be wearing panties," Poochie said smiling. They all busted out laughing.

Kim said, "I know that's right, besides what the hell are you gonna wear Carmen?" Carmen walked towards her bags and sat on the couch.

"Aw you know I went and copped me some *Louis Vuitton* and I got my man some *Polo*. Just a little something, something," Carmen said smiling.

"Y'all want something to drink? I want y'all pissy drunk before y'all come back here tonight. We can all do something," Mack said looking for Carmen's reaction.

"Mack your not working with what you think you are," Kim said. Everybody except for Mack started laughing.

"Oh yeah, the jokes on me huh? I know I'm working with a Tyreks!"

"A Tyreks?" Kim asked.

"Yeah in other words a monster!" Mack said as they laughed even more.

Carmen walked to the bathroom and started getting ready for the night. She sat in the tub and thought about Pinky and what she was doing in Miami. Kim came to the door and told Carmen that Poochie and Mack left to make a run.

"Where did they say they were going?" Carmen asked.

"They didn't say, they just left. I'm about to go home and get dressed. I'll be back in an hour. Do you think I need another touch up?" Kim asked.

"Girl go on, I just did your hair," Carmen replied to her. Kim left out and went home.

Carmen sat in the tub and thought about the come up Montana was about to get. Not really knowing what was going on, but loyalty played a big part.

Carmen got with Juan and Jose during their first trip and discussed some plans about the package and how if it went sweet as Montana said it would go, then with the money Montana spent and the money she would invest, it would be like a front, but in reality it would be theirs.

Montana would only be responsible for what he controlled solely for him, but his loyalty showed at the bar with the strippers. Montana's loyalty was to Carmen.

Carmen gave the call to the driver to go to Cleveland. She was proud of Montana. In her heart he was the one for her. The cool water broke her out of her thoughts as she heard someone saying her name, "Carmen!"

"Yeah I'm in the tub," Carmen said.

"Hey lil' mommie hurry up! I can't wait for you to hook me up with your chica friend Pinky," Jose said laughing in the hallway. Montana walked in the bathroom and gave Carmen a kiss.

"What's up boo? You all sexy in the tub gonna make me get naked up in here," he said.

"That's what's up, what's stopping you?" Carmen said wanting him to get in.

"Girl you know we got company out there, besides you know my shoulder hurting. You showing out, just wait I got you," Montana said smiling.

"That's what's up, did you see the clothes I bought you?" Carmen asked Montana.

"Yeah I seen them, but for some reason I can't find my Kush," Montana said looking for Carmen's reaction.

She smiled and said, "that might be it in the ashtray."

"Did Mack and them come back yet?" he asked.

"Yeah they came back, then him and Poochie went somewhere else. Kim said she was going home to get dressed," Carmen replied.

# Chapter Thirty-Three

## *Mack and Poochie*

"Hello may I speak to Chino? This is P ... Peaches," Poochie said.

"Where I know you from?" Chino asked.

"Dag you forgot me already, you must don't want none of this," Poochie said in a teasing way, "I just gave you my number today in the mall, unless you met so many people today you forgot who I am."

"Oh naw I know who you are sexy. What's up sexy? Where you at?" Chino asked.

"I'm trying to hook up with you, where you at?" Poochie asked flirting with Mack that was sitting right next to her in the car, with a .40 caliber pistol sitting on his lap.

"I'm at the Holiday Inn, why are you coming to see me?" Chino asked Poochie.

"I can, but I can't stay long. I'm going out tonight," Poochie answered.

"Where are you at?" he asked her.

"I'm over my girlfriend's house, but she's getting dressed. I got about an hour to chill with you," Poochie said.

"Well if you're coming now, hurry up! I'm in room 189," he responded.

"Okay Chino, I'm on my way," she said hanging up the phone.

"Look!" Mack said, "I'm gonna go in and make sure everything is clear. When you see me walk back down the hall, you knock on the door. When he opens the door, I'm gone rush in the room. You go back outside to the car. You hear me?"

"I hear you," Poochie said as Mack pulled up in the parking lot and walked in the hotel.

Poochie did exactly what Mack said. The plan couldn't have worked any better. Chino saw Poochie coming down the hallway with the door open, not knowing Mack had set the plan up perfect.

Mack pushed in the suite as Poochie said, "what's going on!" She walked off as Mack upped his hammer.

"Look here, I come no mask to let you know I didn't came to play with you. That disrespect you put down on me with my girl right in front of me ..."

After all was said and done, Mack grabbed an iron cord and tied the bathroom door shut. He walked out the hotel and to the car where Poochie was nervously waiting. He got rid of the phone before he got in the car and drove off. He headed to the hotel.

"Bae you crazy!" Poochie said to him. Mack pulled out the bag of powder and handed it to Poochie.

"Hit this!" Poochie grabbed the bag and sniffed some of the powder and passed it back to Mack. She leaned back and the rush from the powder went straight to her head. Mack took a sniff as he turned into the hotel parking lot, parking the car.

Poochie came out of her zone.

Mack turned to her and said, "don't tell anybody about what just happened!" He looked at the jewelry he took out the bag. Poochie looked in amazement.

"Let me wear this one." Mack looked at her and said, "don't start, I'll look out for you later." They walked in the hotel room.

"Babe here they go. Where y'all been?" Carmen asked Poochie.

Mack spoke up grabbing Poochie's booty, "y'all know me, I had to get mines."

"Mack your so nasty," Kim said making everybody laugh. Poochie grabbed her clothes and walked to the bathroom.

"Hurry up and get dressed y'all!" Carmen said walking back to the front where everyone was at.

"I'm about to get ready too," Mack said as he walked in the bathroom carrying his grab bag and another bag. They both cleaned up.

Poochie went and grabbed her necklace out of her bag. When she came in the bathroom Mack was putting on all the stolen jewelry, looking in the mirror at himself. Poochie asked him what was he doing putting the jewelry on.

"I'm doing what the fuck I want to do!" he said handing her a pill, "here take this." She popped the pill and put her necklace on and walked out the bathroom to where Kim and Carmen stood.

Mack came out the bathroom, shining with his Cleveland Browns outfit on representing the Dawg Pound.

"Damn baller!" Montana said with everyone recognizing the jewels. Kim noticed the jewels off top asked in a low voice, "girl what did y'all do?"

# Chapter Thirty-Four

*Mack*

"Yeah boy, you doing the damn thang!" Montana told Mack. He stood in the middle of the room draped up in jewels.

"Yeah my nigga, life is getting better as we go," Mack said as he looked at himself reflecting off the China cabinet glass, "I'm ready to go and party. We only live once." Everyone stood there looking ready to go.

Poochie came out dressed looking so good that everybody turned their attention to her.

"Damn baby you looking so good in that Cavs dress. I don't even know if I want to go partying," Mack said.

Montana came out the bathroom with his *Polo* outfit on and smoking a blunt, "y'all ready?" he asked.

Jose spoke up, "yeah I been ready to go, I can't wait to see my new girlfriend, Pinky!" Jose said in a funny Spanish accent. Everybody broke out laughing.

"Let's go ball out," Mack said as he tapped Juan on his arm asking him if he had any coke on him, "we trying to zone out before we go," Mack said hugging Poochie.

"Naw man I don't," Juan answered.

"Kim said, "I got a little bit," pulling out the bag of cocaine walking to the backroom. Mack pulled Poochie's arm as they followed Kim and the bag of yayo. When they got to the backroom, Kim looked at Mack and closed the door.

Once the door was closed she asked Mack, "you robbed dude that was at the mall?"

"Hell yeah I robbed that bitch ass nigga! I don't know how niggas down here get down but I'm a real street nigga. I can't accept no pussy ass niggas disrespecting me and they don't pay. These niggas don't know who they fucking with. They gave y'all their number while I'm standing right there. They must be crazy!" Mack said as he grabbed the bag and sniffed the cocaine.

Mack said, "they got me fucked up for real!" Kim sniffed some coke, then passed it to Poochie to get some.

Carmen knocked on the door and said, "Come on y'all we're waiting for y'all!"

When they came out the backroom Montana said, "it's time to celebrate Miami style!"

---KQP---

Club Sin is what the sign to one of the hottest clubs in South Beach, Miami read. Pulling up in front of the club was hard work. There was bumper to bumper traffic and people were everywhere trying to get in the club.

They made their way to the back door and was escorted by two cocky ass bouncers. They paved their way through the crowd. Montana and his crew followed them to the back where Jose and Juan had it set up VIP for them.

They walked through noticing the different people. The women were dressed scantily and they were mostly beautiful.

They heard someone calling Carmen's name. The bouncer stopped the lady from coming through until Jose saw Pinky, giving them the okay for Pinky to roll with them.

They made their way to the back of the club where their table was at. There was food, liquor and bottles of champagne sitting on ice.

They all sat down as different people asked if they could come and chill in VIP with them. Kim and Poochie had on their sexy ass sports dresses. Carmen had on some *Louis Vuitton* short shorts that showed her long pretty legs and the cheeks of her ass. Her *Louis Vuitton* top had her titties fat and that enhanced her long curly hair she had in a braided ponytail. She sat her *Louis Vuitton* purse on the table.

Pinky was wearing an all pink bodysuit, that hugged every cut and curve of her body. She gave Carmen a hug. Carmen introduced her to everybody as Jose reintroduced himself to her by saying, "hey baby."

Pinky's style was crazy pink. Her hair, bodysuit, shoes and contacts were Pink and Jose was feeling it. He moved closer to her as everybody began mingling with each other.

Mack was sitting back sipping a bottle of Moet. Kim and Poochie was flirting back and forth with each other. Montana, Juan and Carmen sat there listening to the music and drinking a bottle of Cristal. Montana rolled some Kush up and passed it around the table.

The club was getting more crowded and it was going hard. There were women dancing on the dance floor shaking it so hard the dudes from the next VIP table got to making it rain. They were throwing all kinds of bills as more and more women got to dancing. They were getting live. The DJ had the party rocking.

When he played *Yo Gotti*, Carmen, Poochie, Pinky and Kim walked out to the dance floor and started dancing. Niggas saw them dancing and everybody wanted to get in. Montana and Jose was on it too. They went to the dance floor and Montana grabbed Carmen and Jose grabbed Pinky. Poochie and Kim played around with some dudes, dancing extra freaky.

"Damn baby, I want some of this," a light brown skinned dude told Poochie trying to freak her booty.

"Watch your hands boo-boo my man is watching us," Poochie responded.

"Okay," the man said looking over to the table where Juan and Mack sat drinking their drinks and feeling the vibe of the music.

Montana and Carmen was going at it on the dance floor. Not only was Carmen fine as hell, Carmen still knew how to dance. She was doing all the latest dances the younger ladies were doing and that was right up Montana's lane. He was a partying ass nigga who loved dancing and Carmen shaking it how she was, had him going.

Pinky was dancing in front of Jose showing her dance moves off. She brought a crowd around her as she made her ass bounce and shake from all different directions.

Carmen, Poochie and Kim came and helped Pinky entertain the crowd. Dudes started going in their pockets, pulling stacks of money out throwing it at them. The crowd got bigger and bigger as they started chanting, "take ... it ... off! Take ... it ... off!" Pinky took a little something off and Poochie raised her dress up to where you could see the thong she was wearing and that made the crowd go crazy. They threw more money at them.

Kim, Carmen, Montana and Jose fell back in the crowd, making their way back to their table. Poochie and Pinky stayed on the dance floor shaking their asses together to the beat as if they've practiced it. They got on their hands and knees and bounced their asses ten minutes straight, making niggas flood them with money.

One of the men watching them asked his friend, "is that the chic we met in the mall today?"

"Yeah that's her shaking her ass," Mike said.

"Let's call Chino," Tee said as he called Chino's hotel to tell him Poochie was in the club.

"Hello," Chino said.

"Chino, I thought you said you were coming to the club, your girl down here."

"Who?" Chino asked.

"The chic we met at the mall today," Tee said.

*"She set me up and got me robbed!"* he responded.

"Robbed!" Tee said, "get the fuck out of here. I'm calling to tell you her and her girl down here getting loose on the dance floor, and you say they robbed you!"

*"Yeah they did! Where y'all at?"* Chino asked.

"We're at Club Sin at South Beach," Tee said.

*"Look I'm about to strap up, don't let that hoe leave!"* Chino said as he got ready to head to the club.

"I won't I'm on her ass for sho' my nigga!" Tee said as he hung up the phone. He told Mike what happened.

"Which one?" Mike asked.

"The one in the Cavs dress," Tee answered, "yeah man she's foul as fuck for that, but you know Chino is about to come down here and act a fool!"

"For sho!" Mike said as he walked closer to where Poochie and Pinky was at.

"Damn baby you tried to get out on me on that dance floor," Montana said to Carmen as he poured them some glasses of Moet.

"What you mean tried?" Carmen asked, "I was out there serving him wasn't I?" Carmen asked Juan with Mack answering the question saying, "hell yeah you was out there handling him. I knew that lil' nigga couldn't work with you!" Mack said laughing.

"Lil' nigga! Who the fuck you talking about!" Montana said in an angry tone.

"Damn my nigga! I didn't mean it like that!" Mack said knowing he overstepped his boundaries.

"Well …" Montana said. Juan stopped him, "Poppi feeling it Montana. This Miami the home of the yayo," he said as he grabbed another bottle of Cristal and popped it open letting some spill to the floor.

"We go hard down here," Juan said looking over to Poochie and Pinky still having the crowd making it rain. Jose stood there faithfully waiting for Pinky and Poochie to finish.

He danced with her, now he wanted her bad. Pinky sensed Jose was ready. She stopped dancing and gathered some of the money up. Poochie followed suit, letting the other ladies take over. Pinky being a pro at chasing paper gathered the bills up without dropping one single bill on the floor.

She made her way to the table with Poochie following her dropping all kinds of bills on the floor.

"Hell yeah," Carmen said giving her props for turning the club out Cleveland style.

"Y'all did y'all damn thing!" Montana said as he opened more bottles of champagne, pouring everybody a glass. Poochie walked over and sat on Mack's lap. Mack gave her a passionate tongue kiss and told her they did a good job as he helped her count the money.

Pinky put all her money in her purse without counting it and went over to Jose. Pinky knew she had him wrapped around her finger. Jose rubbed her three songs straight and she felt the wetness from his pants on her ass. Pinky wanted the money and she knew he had it.

Carmen told her he had it, but he was family. Normally she would rob him, but because of Carmen, she had to keep it fair.

Juan popped another bottle filling everyone's glass up again. Mack was feeling himself for real. In a slurred he stood up wobbling.

"We're coming up Montana, straight from Cleveland!" Mack said. He asked Juan where the men's room was. Juan told Mack that he would go with him. They made their way through the crowd towards the restroom.

Carmen and Poochie followed behind them. They made their way through the crowd not knowing Chino had made his way through the crowd right behind them, with Tee and Mike following him.

Chino saw Mack with all his jewelry on said, "I can't believe this dumb ass nigga had the nerve to rob me and wear my shit to the club the same night!"

Feeling the .45 caliber pistol in his waistband under his shirt. He chuckled to his self as he watched Mack go in the men's room and Carmen and Poochie went in the ladies' room.

Chino told Mike to watch the ladies room. He and Tee walked towards the men's room. Chino pulled the gun out, cocked it and opened the door. Mack had just finished washing his hands when the door swung open and Chino raised his gun at Mack. Juan coming out the stall was close enough to Chino, so he rushed him and pushed him into the door. Chino let three shots off, hitting Juan in the face and chest area. During their tussle Mack and two other men ran past them and out the door quickly blending into the scattering crowd.

Carmen walking past the men's room heard the shots and saw Mack and two other men run past her. With the door opened she looked inside and saw Juan laying on the floor bleeding from the face. She pulled her gun out and shot the man standing in the doorway with a gun in his hand. The crowd scattered everywhere. She made her way back towards Montana and them. Everybody asked her what happened and where was Juan.

"Come on Jose we got to get out of here!" Carmen said trying to leave the club and get away, hearing sirens nearing.

"Where's Juan?" Jose yelled crying as Montana and Mack pulled him towards the back exit.

"He got shot up!" Mack said.

"Shot up for what?" Jose said with fire in his eyes.

"I don't know! I don't know who those dudes was!" Mack said lying about not knowing what happened.

"Carmen what happened?" Jose asked getting in the car.

"I don't know either, I just saw Mack and some other dudes run out the men's room and Juan was on the floor bleeding from the face with a man standing over him with a gun in his hand. That's when I shot him up and ran to y'all!" Carmen said.

"Was he dead?" Jose asked.

"I think so!" Carmen said. Jose jumped out the car and ran back into the club with Kim and Pinky closely following behind him.

Montana, Mack, Poochie and Carmen pulled out the parking lot and headed to the hotel, then to Cleveland.

Montana called Kim and told her to call him if she found anything out. He tried to console her.

She said, "Montana, Mack has something to do with this, he's not right! I'll talk to you later." Kim hung up. Montana headed towards the freeway. He headed I-75 North back to Cleveland.

# Chapter Thirty-Five

### Old Man James and Candy Gurl

"Oooh baby what happened to you?" Candy Gurl asked Old Man James as he walked in the apartment with his face swollen and bloody from the scuffle he had earlier.

"Aw it ain't nothing. You think this is bad wait until you see what I did to CB lil' punk ass!" Old Man James said lying about what happened.

"Y'all was fighting?" Candy Gurl asked.

"Ya damn right we were. This nigga thought I was some type of sucker or something," Old Man James said pulling the rocks out of his pocket and sitting them on the table, "he acted like he wasn't gonna pay me for the work I done. He got me fucked up. I'm a outlaw for real. I might smoke now, but I still got these hands!" Old Man James said throwing a fast fury of punches in the air.

"Boo you should've heard that nigga yelling for me to get off of him. I had his ass on the ground hitting him from all different ways. He didn't know how I was gonna get off of his ass, until five or six people pulled me off of him."

"Baby you shouldn't have did that. You're gonna have every dope boy down the way looking for us," Candy Gurl said, "If CB look like you say he do."

"I'm not worried. That nigga knew he was wrong. That's why after he came to his senses, he paid me the money he owed me." Old Man James said grabbing one of the rocks from the table and breaking It down.

He asked her what she got from Black Dee for helping him. Candy Gurl went in the cabinet where she secured the rocks from herself and put the seven rocks on the table along with Old Man James rocks.

"Damn I see he gave you some boulders huh?" Comparing her rocks to the rocks he had.

"Yeah these boulders for your shoulders," Candy Gurl said laughing.

Old Man James told her to go get her clothes together, so they can move for a couple weeks.

"I think we should move to the west side," Candy Gurl suggested.

"Who you know over there?" Old Man James asked her while going through the few clothes he had.

"That's where Shooter and Juan moved to and they came up," she said.

"Well we got to go somewhere to the sunset because I'm not going to jail," Old Man James said taking a big hit of crack from his pipe blowing the smoke in the air.

"How long do you think it's gonna be until things cool down?" Candy Gurl asked between talking and smoking.

"I don't know … why?" Old Man James asked.

"Because we only got these rocks to live off of and how you smoke …" Candy Gurl said.

Old Man James said in an angry tone, "bitch don't make me finish frying a ass with yours! You got all these muthafucking jokes. Now ain't the time for no bullshit! You better go get your shit ready and don't worry about how much I smoke stanking ass stink bowl!"

"What you call me?" Candy Gurl asked.

"You heard what I said, now go get ready before I leave without you!" He packed two pairs of pants and two t-shirts in a trash bag and he headed towards the door. He was telling Candy Gurl to hurry the fuck up.

"I'm coming!" she said carrying a big trash bag full of dirty clothes with a hooded coat hanging off her head.

"Where the fuck you going with all that dirty shit?" Old Man James asked her.

"I don't got much, but I'm not about to leave my stuff so somebody can steal my shit!"

"Ain't nobody about to steal all of them dirty ass clothes! What they go do steal them and go wash them!" Old Man James said laughing, "now sit that bag and stuff down and go around the corner and ask Israel if he can drive us to the west side."

Candy Gurl sat her stuff down and walked out the apartment building.

"Oh shit!" Candy Gurl said as she walked around the corner where CB, Pimp and Black Dee were standing.

*I hope they don't do nothing to me* she thought to herself as she relived the story Old Man James told her about what happened. Scared she tried to walk past unnoticed. She looked out the corner of her eye at CB.

"Candy Gurl!" She jumped at the sound of CB's voice not knowing whether to run or what.

"Huh?" she said still froze.

"Did you see I kicked yo dude ass for trying to steal?" CB said.

"Naw I haven't seen him since yesterday," she said lying, but looking at CB to see if he had any marks on him.

"Well when you see him, tell him he's not allowed back out here on the strip," CB said as he rubbed his swollen hand carefully.

"Okay," Candy Gurl said as she started back walking towards Israel's apartment building.

*That lying muthafucka* Candy Gurl said to herself laughing hard as hell at Old Man James.

# Chapter Thirty-Six

## *Lil' Shorty*

"Case #552432 Michael Jones," the judge said as Lil' Shorty and his lawyer stepped up.

"This is case #552432 count one attempted murder and count two, felonious assault. This is your arraignment, how do you plea?" Judge Roland asked. Lil' Shorty's lawyer went to working his magic. He told the judge they plead not guilty and they would like to file a motion to suppress the evidence. He also told him that Michael Jones was not an escape risk and he would like a reasonable bond in order to fight the case from the streets.

The judge read his case and without an adult record. He looked at Lil' Shorty and his lawyer.

"I'm setting your bond at $50,000 on count one and $50,000 on count two," the judge said.

Lil' Shorty asked his lawyer, "is that 10%? What about my money?"

"You'll get both of them," the lawyer said.

"Well I need a bondsman to get me out of jail," Lil' Shorty said.

"I'll take care of it today. I need you to bring me another $2,500 for your bond and for me," the lawyer said handing Lil' Shorty a pack of cigarettes as he walked out the courtroom, "I'll see you later."

Lil' Shorty jumped in the air, "yes! I'll be out this muthafucka today."

One of the dudes in the line saw Lil' Shorty get the squares, "aye man you about to get out?"

"Yeah man," Lil' Shorty said not knowing him.

"What are you down for?" he asked Lil' Shorty.

"Why? What's up?" Lil' Shorty asked back.

"Naw it ain't like that, I'm just happy to see you leaving my nigga," he said.

"Well I don't be talking, because niggas be rats telling and I'm not trying to get snitched on!" Lil' Shorty said.

"I know that's right. What lawyer did you have?" the dude asked.

"Paul Manning," Lil' Shorty responded. The dude continued to ask Lil' Shorty all the basic questions about the lawyer. He asked Lil' Shorty where he was from.

"I'm from down the way," Lil' Shorty answered.

"Oh yeah I know a lot of dudes from the bricks. I just went on a move my nigga put me on to," dude responded.

"Straight up!" Lil' Shorty said trying to see what the play was about.

"Yeah we was about to hit for about 200 bands," he said.

"Get the fuck out of here!" Lil' Shorty said.

"Man, I won't lie to you my nigga," the dude said lifting his shirt up from the back showing Lil' Shorty the wounds.

"Damn what the fuck happened right there?" Lil' Shorty asked.

"I told you I went on a lick with a couple of my niggas from down the way and the lick went bad," he responded.

"What happened?" Lil' Shorty asked.

"The niggas I went with didn't know dude had no dogs!" he replied.

"Dogs!" Lil' Shorty said.

"Yeah dogs, we caught the nigga in the cut and just as we got the ups on the nigga, two pits came out the cut attacking us," he continued.

"Then what happened? Y'all let some dogs stop y'all from getting 200 bands. Nothing would have stopped me from getting that paper," Lil' Shorty said still listening closely.

Dude continued, "it was dark and before we could get the last dog to stop, the nigga took off running in the dark. I couldn't shoot the nigga down, but while I was shooting at him somebody opened the back door and got to busting at us. I got hit three times and my big homie got grazed. Man those bullets put me on fire," he said.

"So y'all didn't get the money?" Lil' Shorty asked.

"Hell naw, we're lucky we got away cause the lady, she dumped her whole clip at us, then ran back in the house," he said.

Lil' Shorty got close enough to punch him in the face. When he bent over, Lil' Shorty kneed him in the face until he felt smooshed bones banging up against his knee. He picked him up and slammed him on the floor. He moaned as he tried to yell for help. Shorty got on top of him, punching him with a fury of punches. He begged Lil' Shorty to stop. Lil' Shorty kept punching him.

"Who turned y'all on to this lick!" Shorty said hitting him a few more times.

"My dude Uncle Marcus!" the dude replied.

"Marcus!" Lil' Shorty said.

"Yeah Marcus, I don't know nothing else about him, except that he's from down y'all way and he got that paper. I never even seen him before. I told you I hopped in on somebody else's lick and I got bit up, shot up and my ass kicked," he said.

Shorty punched him again and said, "you better tell me something else or I'm about to kill your ass!" Lil' Shorty continued choking him.

"Alright! Alright! Dee-Dee my people and the niggas that shot him up. One of them came back and turned us on to the lick. I don't know who did what. I just wanted to be a part of the paper, especially after they tried to shoot us up and shot my niggas up in Longwood. I was trying to get money," the dude said crying.

Lil' Shorty punched him again. He pled for help as another man grabbed Lil' Shorty's arm.

"Come on my nigga your about to get out! Don't catch another case!" Two other dudes helped pull Lil' Shorty off of him.

Lil Shorty said, "bitch ass nigga! You better be telling me the truth, because if I don't find this Marcus, if I ever see you again, you know what it is!" Lil' Shorty said as the bailiff came and opened the door calling off names.

When he called Lil' Shorty's name. Lil' Shorty walked out the door into the hallway. The dude Lil' Shorty beat up was coming towards the door with his face swollen and bruised, until the one dude that pulled Lil' Shorty off of dude stopped him by pushing him towards the back of the room.

"What the fuck you trying to do get caught?" the dude asked him.

Lil' Shorty stood in line asking the bailiff where they were going.

The bailiff answered him, "y'all going to y'all blocks until someone pay y'all bonds."

"Why I got to go back upstairs. I know I'm about to get out today," Lil' Shorty told him.

"Well until they come down here and pay your bond. Your going back upstairs and you will be released then," the bailiff responded.

When Lil' Shorty stepped in the pod, a couple of dudes he knew asked him what happened. He picked the phone up and gave Stan the pack of squares and dialed Peaches' number. After the phone rang a few times, she answered the phone.

*"What's up lil' pimp? How are you?"* she asked.

"I'm good, they just gave me a bond and I'm about to get out soon. My people coming down here to get me out," Lil' Shorty responded.

*"I told you that I need to talk to you, so once you get your things together, come and see me, I got some news and some nookie for you,"* Peaches said.

Peaches wanted to make sure he came to see her when he got out. He told her that they would talk about everything that needed to be talked about soon. He hung up and called Montana.

Montana answered the phone, *"hello."*

"Unc what's good?" Lil' Shorty asked Montana.

*"I can't call it, what's up with you?"* Montana responded.

"I just came back from court and they gave me a bond. The lawyer told me to bring him five stacks and he would get me out today. CB already downstairs waiting for me to come back from court, so I'm just waiting to get out. I got some news for you unc. Your gonna love this, but I can't tell you over the phone right now," Lil' Shorty told Montana.

*"What's it's about?"* Montana asked.

"It's about what happened to you!" Lil' Shorty answered.

*"Oh yeah!"* Montana responded excitedly.

"Yeah unc, but I took care of it, now I'm just ready to come up," Lil' Shorty said.

*"Well that's a good thing. I just got back in town, so when you get out, you come straight over here, it's that time,"* Montana said. Lil' Shorty knowing he was about to be blessed, smiled to himself.

"Unc you know I'm ready for whatever!" Lil' Shorty said. The turnkey said, "Michael Jones rag and bag!"

"Unc they're calling me to be released! I'll get with you in a minute," Lil' Shorty said.


---KQP---


After going through process Lil' Shorty got released. CB and Black Dee was standing outside in front of a blue 2007 Lexus LS.

"Damn whose car is this?" Lil' Shorty asked as CB waved his keys in the air.

"Oh this his, I got the '08," CB said pointing to the all-white Lexus LS parked a few cars down.

"I see y'all out here going hard!" Lil' Shorty said proudly.

"Yeah man, you know we got to put on for the city!" Black Dee said smiling with his front eight all gold.

"Man what the fuck!" Lil' Shorty said grabbing Dee's face to look at his teeth.

"I told you I'm coming up!" Black Dee said smiling.

"I see," Lil' Shorty responded still smiling.

CB said, "you got a bag of money in there," referring to the money he owed him, plus from the stuff he took from Old Man James.

"I told you about Old Man James," CB said laughing.

"Yeah you said that, but your swollen face is telling me something different," Lil' Shorty said laughing, "while we're sitting here bullshitting, I got to go over unc house. I know y'all should be ready to cop some work," Lil' Shorty continued.

"Man I was hoping you said that because I made every dime I could make off of the stuff I had," CB said.

"Let me use one of these cars and I'll be back soon as I finish," Lil' Shorty said. CB tossed him the keys and said, "be careful because that's luxury," CB said laughing referring to his car.

"I got you my nigga!" Lil' Shorty got in the car and pulled out the parking lot headed towards Montana's house. Lil' Shorty picked CB's phone up off the seat and dialed Peaches' number.

When she answered he said, "what's up baby, I'm out."

*"Hey there lil' pimp! Where are you at? Is you on your way over here?"* she asked.

"I'm about to go take of something and when I finish that, then I'm coming to get you, okay?" he replied to her.

*"Okay,"* Peaches answered.

"Oh yeah, what did you have to tell me?" Lil' Shorty asked.

*"I'll tell you when you get over here, right now, I'm about to get in the tub and freshen up before you get here,"* she said flirtingly.

"Okay," Lil' Shorty said. He hung up the phone and cut CB's sounds up to *Drake's Started from the Bottom.* He was thinking to his self, *I'm about to come up.*

# Chapter Thirty-Seven

## Carmen

After touching down from Miami, Carmen sat in the front seat of Montana's car pleading to drop Mack and Poochie off at their own apartments.

She thought to herself, *damn I can't believe we were just enjoying life and now my dude is dead and I killed a man this can't be life.* She continued to think about how things played out.

She turned to Mack and faced him and asked, "I know I asked you before but what happened again?"

Mack looked at her and said, "I just finished washing my hands when Juan came out of the stall. I looked in the mirror as a man came through the door with a gun in his hand. He said y'all know what this is. When I turned around they just started shooting. Juan jumped in front of me and rushed the man as he shot two more times. I ran past him and the next thing I know I looked back hearing shots and the shooter was laying on the floor, that's all I seen."

"So you have never seen the shooter before?" Carmen asked.

"Naw I never seen dude before," Mack responded.

Poochie looked out the side of her eye at Carmen. Montana was looking out the window. Montana pulled up to Mack's apartment and let him out the car. Montana told Mack that he would be to see him in about an hour. Mack got out the car kissing Poochie.

"I'll see y'all later," Mack got out his car and walked into his apartment. Montana pulled off and headed towards Poochie's apartment.

Carmen knew Poochie knew something. She wanted to talk to her, but she knew it wasn't the time.

"Come up to the shop later," Carmen told Poochie as Montana pulled up to her apartment. Poochie got out of the car and grabbed her clothes from the trunk and walked in her apartment.

Once Carmen and Montana were alone Carmen turned to him and said, "babe I think Mack had something to do with what happened with Juan."

"How do you think that?" Montana asked.

"Because when we were leaving out the club, Kim was yelling that Mack did something, but I was in such a hurry to get up out of there. I didn't hear what she said and when I asked him what happened he said some dudes tried to rob them, but Poochie gave me a look."

"A look!" Montana said.

"Yeah, she been acting as if she knows something, but she can't say right now, then I tried to call Kim, but she won't answer her phone. Babe it's a lot of stuff happening and we got to make sure we get shit together, 'cause I'm trying to live for the long haul. I'm gonna go home for a minute, but I got to go up to the shop and make sure everything's going okay. I know you got a lot to do since Jose sent his driver up here. He is on his way over here to see you. While you're taking care of business, I'm gonna go and see my girls at the shop. I haven't been there in a while and I miss my baby," she said referring to the shop.

Her phone rang several times. Carmen answered, "hello."

*"Hey girlfriend,"* Cream answered.

"Hey what's up," Carmen answered.

*"Girl I been up here in Cleveland all week waiting to get my hair done. Where you at?"* Cream asked.

"I'm so sorry, I just got in from Miami this morning, but I'm about to go up to the shop right now," Carmen replied.

*"Damn baller! I see you going everywhere but Cali, how is that?"* Cream asked.

"Girl, I can't lie though, I miss you. It's been just so much going on lately, that I'm trying to find out what it is. I'm sorry though," Carmen continued.

*"Well you know if you need me to come and cut a muthafucka up, I will!"* Cream said laughing.

Carmen busted out laughing and said, "Naw I don't need that shit girl! I'm about to go to the shop right now, so I'll see you when you get up there."

Carmen walked in the house without the happiness of Kilo and Kush. Carmen picked up her phone and dialed a number.

*"Hello,"* a lady answered.

"Hey girl," Carmen responded, "did anything happen while I was gone?"

*"Yeah it was some investigator looking through your yard. They picked some things up off the ground and went through your trash cans. I don't know what they were doing, but they had a dog walking around sniffing and they took some pictures,"* the lady informed Carmen.

"Okay girl, thank you for looking out for me," Carmen said.

*"You know I'm gonna look out for my niece,"* Carmen's aunt Joy said.

Carmen hung up the phone. She told Montana about the investigators that came and checked the yard. She told him that it wouldn't be good to do anything at the house, knowing people were watching the house.

Carmen walked into the bedroom and changed her clothes. She grabbed the Kush that was on the dresser and rolled herself a blunt. She grabbed her bag and walked towards the door. She fired her blunt up once she got in the car.

As she was smoking the blunt, her phone rang. When she answered the phone it was Kim saying, *"Carmen Mack got my brother killed!"*

"What you mean Mack got your brother killed?" Carmen asked.

*"He robbed that man!"* Kim yelled.

"What man?" Carmen asked.

Kim began to tell Carmen about when her, Poochie and Mack were in the mall and how her and Poochie met Chino and his friends and how Mack watched them exchange numbers.

*"The guy Poochie exchanged numbers with, had on these gold chains, bracelet and watch that Mack had on. Kim told Carmen that Mack only had enough money to buy the chain he bought Poochie."*

"That must be where they came from after they came back to get dressed," Carmen chimed in, "because Mack came out the bathroom with all those chains on."

*"Yeah so when we got to the club, Mack had on all dude's stuff. Somebody must have noticed and called Chino and that's when he came and saw Mack and Juan going into the bathroom,"* Kim continued telling Carmen.

"Yeah because Mack just told me the guy came straight in there saying, lay it down and started shooting. Why shoot if you're robbing somebody!" Carmen said.

Kim replied, *"they came shooting because they wanted Chino's shit back! You know Juan ain't go let nobody he with get hurt, if he can help it!"*

"That dirty muthafucka!" Carmen said, "I got him!"

---KQP---

*Ring Ring Ring* … "Hello Montana, what's good big baby?" Mack asked as he sat in the car smoking a blunt.

*"What's up Mack? Where you at?"* Montana responded.

"I'm right here off Kinsman, what's up?" Mack answered.

*"Hey come through I got something for you,"* Montana told him.

"I'm on my way," Mack said as he turned around and headed towards Montana's house. When Mack pulled up Montana came straight out and jumped in the front seat with a bag in his hand. He told Mack to drive around the block. He handed him the bag and told him it was three kilos in it. Mack pulled back around in front of Montana's house and Montana got out of Mack's car.

"I still need to talk to you," Montana told Mack.

"I'll call you later," Mack responded as he pulled off headed towards Poochie's apartment.

When he got to Poochie's apartment, he called her and told her to open the door. He got out the car with the bag in his hand. He walked into her apartment and placed the bag on the table. He asked Poochie what she was doing.

He opened the bag and one of the cases. Poochie walked in the kitchen, and Mack began to sniff some of the powder from the open case.

"Damn this is some fire!" he said offering Poochie some. She sniffed some and the rush hit her instantly. She closed her eyes and gathered her thoughts for a second. When she opened her eyes, Mack reached up and slapped her in the face.

"Bitch you think I didn't see you cut your eyes when Carmen was asking me what happened!"

"Mack I didn't cut my eyes!" Poochie said. Mack slapped her again and she fell into the corner.

"Mack I love you! I'll never do nothing to hurt you. I been doing everything you tell me to do and you still don't show me no love!" Poochie said walking upstairs crying.

"Bring your ass back down here!" Mack said sniffing some more powder out of his hand. He held his hand out so Poochie could sniff some. Mack grabbed her and pulled her close. He started kissing and caressing her, then he wiped the tears from her face. He slowly pulled her clothes off and walked her into the front room. He laid her on the floor and kissed and rubbed all over her, until she moaned.

"Make love to me. I want to have your baby. I want you to love me like I love you." She grabbed him and pulled him close. She started kissing, caressing and hugging him. She began to cry on him.

190

Though Mack was hard on her, he did have feelings for her and somewhat cared for her. He took off his clothes and started making love to her. They laid on the floor going at each other.

Poochie told him, "let's go into the bedroom and finish this." Mack got up with Poochie right behind him. They went into the kitchen and sniffed some more powder. Poochie put some water in the coffee pot and cut the stove on and headed upstairs to finish making love.

Poochie laid on the bed and Mack climbed on top of her to finish his thing. They laid there and Mack asked, "do you smell something?"

Poochie replied, "oops! I forgot I left the stove on!" Poochie got up and ran downstairs with Mack right behind her. The kitchen was smoky, but there was no fire. They cut the stove off.

Mack gathered his coke and put his clothes on. Poochie went back upstairs and ran some bathwater.

Mack's phone rang and he answered, "hello."

*"Mack what's good big homie?"* the caller asked.

"Who is this?" Mack asked.

"This Bus."

"What's up?" Mack responded.

"Man I need you to holla at me."

"Where you at?"

"I'm in the Wood." Mack asked him what did he have.

"I got four stacks on me right now." Mack told him to meet him in the cut in five minutes. He put some of the powder in a small baggie eye balling it to determine how much it weighed and then put it in his pocket. He walked through the back door and made his way through the cut.

Mack was going through a lot of coke and his problems was turning for the worse. He knew Montana had been in the streets for a long time and sooner than later someone would tell him about the lick he tried to set up. Montana's right hand man. He still envied Montana because he felt like if it wasn't for him, they wouldn't be on.

It was Mack that first met Carmen and if Montana wasn't around it would've been him with her. Mack was tired of everyone saying Montana.

*Where's Montana, give this to Montana. Fuck Montana!* he thought to himself. His nose began to run from snorting all the coke, *Fuck Montana!* he continued to think to himself.

Hearing Mack leave, Poochie ran down the stairs and locked her back door. She heard Mack's conversation on the phone. She went in the kitchen and grabbed the bag of cocaine and went into the closet and grabbed the bloody sweatshirt and grabbed a bigger bag. She ran out of her apartment and down the street. When she got to the corner of her street, she ran right in from of a car screaming, "please help me!"

The lady was shocked and scared. When she came to her senses she opened her passenger door letting Poochie in and the big bag she was carrying into the car and she pulled off without looking back.

Poochie went to work on the lady, telling her to, "drive, drive please!" The lady drove faster while asking Poochie what happened.

"My boyfriend just beat me up and raped me!" Poochie told the lady. The lady asked Poochie if she wanted her to take her to the hospital or to the police station. Poochie told her no thank you and that she would be okay as long as she got away from him. The lady looked at her as to say, are you sure.

Poochie wiped her tears away and said, "if you could take me to the west side over my sister's house, I'll be okay."

The lady made her way to the west side of Cleveland heading up Lorain Avenue. Poochie looked out the window and saw Candy Gurl and Old Man James walking down the street.

"Stop right here!" Poochie said pointing at Candy Gurl and Old Man James, "that's my sister right there, I'll be good right here. Thank you for your help."

Poochie grabbed her bag and got out the car. She called Candy Gurl's name. Hearing her name being called she looked around and saw Peaches. Candy Gurl ran over to Peaches.

"Girl what are you doing way over here?" Candy Gurl asked her.

"Girl I just seen y'all," Peaches said, "where y'all going?" she asked.

"You heard what that detective said that night right? I'm no trying to go to jail," Old Man James said.

"Me neither!" Peaches agreed.

"We got a motel room, but we are about to go get something to eat, Candy Gurl told Peaches, "you want to go?"

"I want to go, but I want to drop my bag off and make some calls," Peaches replied adjusting the bag she was carrying.

"I'll carry it until we get back to the motel," Old Man James said. They continued walking down the street.

"We got some rocks if you need a hit," Candy Gurl said offering Peaches some crack.

"I haven't had nothing to smoke in over a week."

"I haven't seen you in over a week," Candy Gurl responded.

"I know I've been in and out of town with my friend." Poochie asked Old Man James if she and Candy Gurl can go back to the motel, while he go and get the food.

"Listen I'm about to go get this food, but I don't want y'all fucking with my shit!" Old Man James said thinking about the last three rocks he had left, "y'all know it costs to live in that room."

"Okay," Peaches said. Her and Candy Gurl turned around and made their way back to the motel room.

"Girl I haven't seen Lil' Shorty all week. They say he been in jail ever since the day they arrested him with James," Candy Gurl said.

"Well I just talked to him today, he's out of jail. I'm about to call him when I get to the motel," Peaches replied. A car blew its horn at them slowing down.

"Ooh that's a lick right there!" Candy Gurl said.

"We cool," Peaches responded.

"Girl you keep some money and stuff. I need to start getting high like you do, because I can't keep being broke," Candy Gurl said laughing as she opened the door to the motel room. Peaches went straight to the bathroom with her bag in her hand.

"Girl I'm not going to go through your stuff. Why are you taking your bag in the bathroom with you?"

Peaches opened the bag and pulled out an open package and walked out the bathroom with it in her hand showing Candy Gurl.

"What's that?" Candy Gurl asked smiling, "where you get that? Is that real? Girl somebody is going to fuck you up." Peaches dumped some on the table.

"That's yours," Peaches said as she poured some more on the table for herself, putting it to the side. She put the rest in her bag and stashed the rest away in a safe place. She told Candy Gurl not to tell anyone what she had.

Candy Gurl hurried up and put hers away. Separating what she was going to show Old Man James and Peaches did the same thing.

Peaches pulled her phone out and called Lil Shorty's phone. The phone rang a few times and Lil' Shorty picked up.

*"Hello,"* Lil' Shorty answered.

"Hey lil' pimp, I need to see you. I got something to tell you," Peaches replied.

*"I'm busy right now, but I'll be with you soon. Call me back."*

---KQP---

Montana sat at his kitchen table. He had the duffle bag sitting on the table. There were eight kilos left after Montana gave Mack his three. Montana was back in the city for about four hours and his phone was ringing off the hook with customers. He continued to sit there waiting on Lil' Shorty to get there. He thought about all the situations that was happening the last few months.

*Wow!* he thought, *I got to come up so I can build a better life for myself and my girl.* He thought about all the things Carmen had did for him and went through. *Damn,* he laughed to himself as he thought about all the times Carmen has shot at people for him. *I'm having sex and making love to a real live hit girl,* he continued to laugh to himself.

Montana began to separate orders from what he had for Lil' Shorty. Things were going good as far as the drug trade was concerned, but Mack's name was starting to pop on some fishy shit.

Montana didn't want to get caught behind someone else's bullshit. He thought about parting ways with him. Montana felt he at least had to have a sit down with him and tell him what it was about. His phone rang. When he answered the phone it was Lil' Shorty telling him he was outside waiting for him.

Montana opened all the dope up into his duffle bag and went outside and got into CB's car that Lil' Shorty was driving.

"What's up nephew," Montana said as he put the bag in the trunk of the car and got in.

"I can't call no shots. I'm happy to be free," Lil' Shorty said. He asked Montana where they were going.

"Down to your house," Montana answered.

"You know right before I got out of jail I had to kick this nigga's ass for trying to rob you!"

"What!" Montana said wanting to know more.

"Yeah I was just coming from court and I was sitting in the bullpen when this nigga get to talking to me, asking me all these different questions. At first I wasn't on it until he asked me if I was from down the way. I said yeah and he got to telling me how he went on a lick for 200 bands."

"Straight up! Who was it?" Montana asked.

Lil' Shorty continued, "he didn't say his name, but he told me some old school name Marcus turned Dee-Dee people onto the lick the same day they got shot up in Longwood. He told me everything that happened. After he told me about Kush and Kilo biting his ass up, he pulled his shirt up and showed me the bullet wounds where he got shot at. That's when I got to kicking his ass. I punched him every which way I could. I was kicking him all in his face. That's when he told me about Marcus."

"I think he was talking about Mack!" Montana said as they pulled up in front of Lil' Shorty's apartment building, "If that's Mack, I'm gonna fuck him up," Montana said walking into Lil' Shorty's apartment with the bag of kilos.

"Look nephew, I'm trying to come up. Now is not the time for us to be playing any games. I need you to be on top of your game, because nothing last forever," Montana said. He pulled a kilo out the bag and handed it to Lil' Shorty.

"You know shit is hot out here and our names are out here ringing bells. Make sure you're laying low and be careful, because this right here is a life sentence. Make sure your moves are calculated, because if there are any holes in our boat we are going to sink for sure."

Lil' Shorty opened the package and got to putting it together. While he was doing that Montana called some of his people back letting them know he was ready to take care of business. He still had a pain in his shoulder, but he knew he needed to take care of business.

Montana made several more phone calls. He knew his house was hot or maybe was under surveillance. He knew he couldn't bring anyone to the house. Montana finished making his calls.

He thought about how much he would make off his package after giving out what he gave out. He estimated that he would be a couple hundred thousand up. He was cool with making something out of that, but he knew that before he got out of the game, he would have to take care of all loose ends.

Though the police had picked Lil' Shorty up and they wanted to know what was going on in the streets, he didn't think that anything would stick to him.

Mack is what really bothered him and if it had to be, he would have to take care of him, because he wasn't worth going to jail for life for.

Mack was using coke and he knew all of Montana's business. It was a high possibility that Mack could be Montana's downfall to the come up he was putting down.

Montana sat there trying to think of what he would do. Montana's phone rang. He answered the phone and it was Mack.

*"Montana ..."* Mack said when he answered.

# Chapter Thirty-Eight

## *Lil' Shorty*

Lil' Shorty sat there after hooking his packages up and dropping them off to all his crew workers. Things were looking good for him. He had got out of jail and just like that everything had finally fell into his lap, like it should have.

After the sit down he had with Montana, he knew he had to lay low for real. Before he went to jail he remembered what Old Man James was telling him about what the detectives said and being out on bond, he knew things were still hot in the projects.

He caught a little feeling in his pants. *Oh yeah,* he thought as Peaches popped up in his head in several different ways. She called him earlier and told him that she needed to and wanted to talk to him. Lil' Shorty thought about taking care of everything in one wop.

He picked his phone up and dialed her number. It rang a couple of times before she answered. Peaches told Lil' Shorty that she was on the west side at a motel with Old Man James and Candy Gurl. She told him that she needed to talk to him in person.

Lil' Shorty got in the car and headed to where Peaches was at. When he pulled up to the motel room he called her phone. Peaches came outside and got in the passenger's seat with a bag in her hand. She told him to pull off.

"Where we going?" Lil' Shorty asked her. She told him she wanted to go somewhere safe. He looked at her with a strange look on her face.

"I want to sit you down and let you know what's going on and what I been going through and where I'm trying to be," Peaches said looking at him with sincerity in her eyes.

Lil' Shorty drove until he reached the Marriot Hotel. He asked her was the hotel safe enough, with a smirk on her face.

They got out of the car and got a room. Once they got in the room Lil' Shorty looked at Peaches and asked, "now that we're alone, what's going on girl?"

"Well let me tell you that I really, really like you. I'm starting … since the first day I met you I wanted to change and be with you and the reason why I'm standing here is because, I'm hoping that after I tell you what I'm about to say, you will believe me and we can make something out of this situation. First let me tell you the bad part, my name is not Peaches." Lil' Shorty raised his eyebrow as she finished, "it's Poochie, I said that because I was out in the streets with Candy Gurl and them. I didn't want you to judge me, or run a check on me in the hood. I'm really a good girl," she said, "now remember I said I had something to tell you?" Lil' Shorty nodded his head yes.

"Well one night when me and Old Man James walked to the Compound we got arrested and I got caught with some of the dope I bought from you. I never went to jail for that, or told nobody, but they asked me some questions and told me if I didn't want to go to jail, I had to find out some information about all them shootings that's been happening lately on Case Court and in Longwood. They also wanted me to tell them where that pure cocaine was coming from."

Lil' Shorty asked, "what did you say?"

"I never said nothing. I got the detective card, but I never called them, so I might have a case," she said smiling.

"So what's the other part?"

"Well I was fucking with this dude and he was treating me bad. He was cheating on me, fighting me and doing his own thing. We was traveling back and forth out of town moving drugs and he wasn't breaking me off nothing. I just couldn't take it anymore, that's when I met you. I seen more and wanted more. After this last trip with him, I made my mind up about what I wanted to do."

"What's that?" Lil' Shorty asked.

"Remember when I told you I was gonna get you some money. Well after the dude I was messing with fought me again, he left out my house and he left this." She went into the bag and pulled two and half kilos out the bag and showed it to him.

"What the fuck!" Lil' Shorty said realizing that it was the same package he just got from Montana.

"Who you get this from?"

"I told you I got it from my ole dude."

"Who!" Lil' Shorty said.

"His name Mack," Poochie said.

"Get the fuck out of here!" Lil' Shorty said going through the package.

"Why you say that? So you know him?"

"If this is who I think it is, he be with my uncle."

"He be with Montana."

"Oh yeah that's my uncle, he goes with Carmen."

"That's who I just came from out of town with. We travel back and forth from Miami all the time." They sat there in deep thought.

Poochie broke the silence, "so is that going to stop us, or what are we gonna do?" Poochie asked breaking the silence.

"I think we got something going on here," Lil' Shorty said. "you know I just got out of jail," he continued while smiling.

---KQP---

Sitting at the top of Case Court in an all-black '99 Ford Taurus, was the head detective of narcotics Jeff Folley and his partner of ten years Leonard Wayne of the third district. They sat in the car looking down the dark one way, observing the drug traffic.

They had been tipped off by a CRI that a black male by the name of Montana Jones was selling large amounts of crack cocaine from 469 Woodland Avenue.

# Chapter Thirty-Nine

## *Mack*

Mack was coming back to Peaches' apartment, after selling Bus the work. Mack thought about the package and the money he was gonna make. Though he knew he would have to find a new connect soon, he was gonna get the getting while the getting was good.

When he got to the door and tried to open it up it, it was locked. He knocked again, but this time a little harder.

He thought to himself, *I can't believe this shit, I know this bitch ain't dumb enough to play me, if so, then she's dumb enough to get herself killed.*

He picked up a brick and broke her windows out and went into her apartment. Mack called her name as he looked through and ransacked her apartment while looking for his cocaine. After not finding what he was looking for, he went into her closet to get the bag he left in there, only to find it was also gone.

He opened the front door, looked out of it, then ran down the street hoping to catch Poochie. She was nowhere to be found as Mack yelled out, "you dirty bitch, you scandalous muthafucka. After all I did for your dope fiend ass. Bitch! When I catch your ass, I got you!"

He walked back toward her apartment and got back in his car. He circled the block hoping that he'd see her. Once he didn't see her he tried calling her phone several times, only to get her voicemail. After leaving several dirty messages on her voicemail, Mack called Montana to tell him what happened.

Mack went to his house and got his gun. As he rode around, he was thinking of where Poochie could be and who or what could have made her do that to him. He finally realized that she was gone in the wind.

He drove to Longwood and copped a sack of Kush to ease his mind. Once he copped the sack, he headed towards Case Court to meet up with Montana. Mack picked his phone up and called Montana's phone.

*"Hello,"* Montana answered.

"Yo! Where you at?" Mack asked.

*"I'm on Case Court,"* Montana answered.

---KQP---

After making all his moves through the city, Montana was sitting in the living room of one of his safe houses he had, counting the money he made from the cocaine.

Once he counted the $92,000 he went and laid in his old bed. An elderly woman came into his room and asked him if he was okay.

"Yeah," he said. Ms. Lucy is Sue and Montana's mother. She raised them by herself after their father was killed in a bar fight when Montana was six and Sue was 12 years old. She never moved out of the house her husband bought for her on E. 61st Street off of Quincy Avenue.

Montana tried several times to move his mother, but she loved her house and the neighborhood. Though it was considered to be in a rough and ghetto area, she was content with what she had. Montana got over trying to move her and just fixed her entire house up, including his childhood bedroom.

This was his home. As he laid on the bed his phone rang, it was Mack calling, *"hello,"* Mack said.

"Yeah what's up?" Montana responded.

*"I need to talk to you. Where you at?"*

"I'm in the bricks, what's up?"

*"Man, meet me on Case in 20 minutes, this bitch Poochie stole my shit!"*

"What shit?"

*"The shit we did!"*

"Get the fuck out of here! How did she do that and where is she at?"

*"I don't know where she at. We was over her apartment getting it on when I got a call. I left out of her spot for a minute and when I came back, her door was locked and she and my shit was gone!"*

"I'll be around there in a minute," Montana said. He put his money up in his safe and left out of his mother's house and headed towards Case Court. When he got close to Case Court, Lil' Shorty called his phone.

"Hello," Montana answered.

*"Unc where you at?"* Lil' Shorty asked.

"I'm on my way to Case Court, why what's up?"

*"Well remember I was telling you about the chic that go hard that I wanted you to meet. Well when I met her she told me her name was Peaches and she danced for a living and wanted to help me get some money, because she was feeling me. Well I got out and hooked up with her. She sat me down and dropped her life story on me. Come to find out that her name ain't Peaches her name is Poochie."*

"Poochie!" Montana said, "Mack girl Poochie, where she at?"

*"She at our hotel room waiting for me,"* Lil' Shorty said.

"Well, Mack is looking for her right now as we speak," Montana replied.

*"I know that's what I'm telling you, she told me about her and Mack and how he turned her out to cocaine and had her doing this and that and how he was doing her wrong. She was telling me that I was a good dude and that she could see herself building with and living for. She also told me what she did to Mack. She gave me his shit to get on my feet with, so I'm sitting right here with everything he had."*

"Get the fuck out of here!"

*"I won't lie to you unc, I'm sitting right here with everything."*

"Well I need to see you, because I'm on my way to Case Court to talk to the nigga right now about the shit that's been going on. Look I want you to give that shit back, it's over with for him. I'm not fucking with him no more," Montana said.

*"Unc man fuck dude! How are you gonna look out for him knowing how foul he is."*

"One thing that's for certain, what you reap is what you sow, so if he got something that's coming to him. It's gonna happen anyway. I been around far too long to know what you do in the dark will always come to the light. If it's meant to be, it will be," Montana told Lil' Shorty hanging up the phone. Montana called Carmen's phone.

"Hello what's up baby," Montana asked.

Carmen answered, *"hey there, what's going on."*

"This is some crazy stuff happening."

*"What happened?"*

"Well you know your girl Poochie, she was calling herself Peaches when she met Lil' Shorty. They must've been messing around for a minute because she's head over hills in love with him."

*"What! I thought she was in love with Mack."*

"That's what I thought until I just heard she stole all of Mack's shit and gave it to Lil' Shorty."

*"For real?"*

"Yeah, that's the same thing I said. I'm on my way over to Case Court right now."

*"What are you gonna do?"*

"I'm going to go get him his shit back and I'm not gonna fuck with him no more."

*"What Lil' Shorty say about that?"*

"He told me fuck him and he got what he deserved. He don't want me to give nothing back."

*"Well I'm down for whatever you down for."*

Carmen asked Montana what time he was going to the Comfort Inn. That's what they called Montana's mother's house.

"When I get all this shit together."

*"Well y'all be careful,"* Carmen said ending the call. Montana hung up the phone as he turned on Case Court.

There was a black Taurus parked almost at the corner of the street. Montana didn't pay attention or notice the two white male police officers that had ducked down when they saw his car pass by.

Once he got in front of Lil' Shorty's apartment building, he called Mack's phone.

*"Hello,"* Mack answered.

"Where you at?" Montana asked. Mack blew his horn letting him know he was right behind him. Montana got out of his car and walked into Lil' Shorty's apartment with Mack following right behind him.

Lil' Shorty was already sitting at the kitchen table with the bag that contained Mack's cocaine inside. When they sat down Mack said, "man I can't believe this bitch played me like that!"

Montana laughed and said, "look, I been telling you that I need to talk to you anyway, so now this is a good time to get everything out in the air. There's the dope."

Mack grabbed the bag and looked inside seeing the two kilos and one opened kilo like he had it.

"How you ..." Mack began to say.

Montana cut him off and finished what he was saying, "like I was saying, that's yours. Poochie who my nephew met as Peaches gave those to him. Luckily he knew it was some of ours or your ass would be shit out of luck. Now back to you, you know I got word that it was you that turned Dee-Dee people onto us."

"I didn't ..." Mack began to speak as Montana cut him off again, "all we been through and you send some niggas at us. No wonder they got past Kilo and Kush, it was you who set it up. I know nobody knew where our spot was at. The first time somebody tried to get at Carmen. It was you who stole dude's jewelry down there. Now you're doing coke and falling for all these trick ass hoes. This it, there's nothing we can ever do together again." Montana said in an angry voice.

Mack responded, "what about you Mon ... tan ... a ... Everybody wants Montana. Had it not been you, I would have been with Carmen. I would have the connect and it would be me putting niggas on. You got my hoes thinking I work for you!" Mack stuck his finger in the cocaine and got a nice blow. I started sniffing from being stressed out around you!" Mack continued yelling, "I'm my own muthafucking man! I don't need you Mon ... tan ... a! I'm on myself! I put in work. I know how to get to Miami myself, I don't need you!"

Some loud knocks banged on the front door got their attention. Lil' Shorty heard the banging and ran to the front door and peeked through the peephole and seen Israel in a panic. Lil' Shorty yanked the door open.

Israel said, "they're coming!"

"Who?" Lil' Shorty asked. He looked down the flight of stairs to see Folley and Ramsey running up the stairs. He tried to close the door, but it was too late. Five or six police and detectives rushed in. Mack tried to get rid of one of the kilos.

"Who shit this belong to!" the detective said looking at Montana.

"Get on the floor!" Everybody got on the floor!" They asked whose apartment it was. The slim white detective wearing a grey t-shirt, jeans and tennis shoes asked. No one answered. Once they were handcuffed, they were put in the unmarked car.

---KQP---

Detective Folley and his partner Officer Thompson sat patiently in the black Taurus. They had been watching the apartment building and they saw the three guys who look to be the suspects. They called for the warrant.

---KQP---

Once they were handcuffed and secured and read their rights, the detective walked in Montana's face and said, "I told you I was going to catch you."

Montana looked at him and said, "do your job!"

The police searched the apartment from top to bottom. They found drugs in all the rooms and put them beside the drugs that was on the table.

After the search, they were all shipped to different precincts. Different detectives came and asked everyone if they had anything to say except Montana.

Israel took off up top and said that he was just the look out and he was there to warn them that the police was about to execute a warrant at the apartment.

They were all shipped from the precincts to the County Jail, where they all had bond hearings. Behind the scene Lil' Shorty was telling Mack that he gave his work back, so he should be responsible for taking out for the two kilos that was found in plain view.

The feds came and tried to get everybody to tell on each other, but the lawyers they had was working against the search warrants and probable cause and the Feds left it up to the State of Ohio.

They all were in the County Jail waiting to get indicted. Montana knew the deck was stacked against him, because Detective Folley had a personal grudge against him. They were from two different worlds and had different ways of life, so coming face to face was like a Holyfield/Tyson fight. They were at each other's throat in every way they could be, with Montana up against the wall fighting for his freedom.

Detective Folley thought he had him down for the count. He went to Mack, Lil' Shorty and Israel to see if they would help him get Montana. Israel folded after seeing the indictment with the two counts and the major drug offender specification.

Meanwhile, everybody else held their balls with the said indictment. They sat in the County month after month waiting to see how the cases they had would play out.

# Chapter Forty

*Carmen*

Carmen had got off the phone with Montana and started taking care of her customers. They talked inside of *Ladies First.* They were informing her on what was going on while she was in Miami. Bay-Bay was putting his extras on Tara's management skills. He had Carmen and everyone inside the hair salon in tears laughing.

CB and Black Dee walked in the shop with frantic looks on their faces.

"Carmen let me holla at you," CB said. Carmen excused herself and walked outside with them.

"What's up?" Carmen asked.

"Brace yourself." She grabbed her face and said, "what is it!"

"I don't know if you know what happened, but Montana, Lil' Shorty, Mack and the fiend Israel just got raided in Lil' Shorty's apartment a few minutes ago."

"Swear!" Carmen told Woo to finish her customer's hair. She grabbed her keys and ran out the shop to her car. She picked her cellphone up and called their lawyer as she was pulling up to the scene.

When she got there, the police had just put them all in separate cars. She ran up to the car that Montana was sitting in the back seat of. The police told her to back away from the car. She was trying to tell the lawyer on the phone what was going on. She was giving him the play by play, but the detectives nor the police would tell her what was found, or who was responsible for what.

She asked them what district they were taking them to. The detectives told her that it would be likely they would go to the 6$^{th}$ district. They pulled off leaving her on Case Court crying.

CB grabbed her and told her that things were gonna be okay. After getting herself together she went home and waited for Montana to call.

To ease her mind, she started cleaning up.

Her phone rang, *"Carmen hey girl,"* Poochie said as Carmen caught her voice. Carmen went the fuck off on her.

"Bitch! You did that stupid ass shit. You then got my muthafucking man caught up, because of the stupid shit you did. They got caught trying to sort out the bullshit!"

*"I didn't mean to cause you no harm Carmen. I swear I didn't. I look up to you!"*

"Bitch! You did!" Carmen said hanging up the phone in Poochie's face. She laid on the couch and started to cry until she fell asleep.

---KQP---

Carmen woke up to the sound of her phone ringing. She hopped up and answered it. It was a collect call from Montana. She accepted the call. She asked Montana if he was okay and what happened. He told her that they supposedly had a search warrant for him and Lil' Shorty at his address and they found some stuff (speaking in code).

*"I don't know what they gonna do though,"* he said, *"besides that, I'm okay. How is you?"*

Carmen told him that she was hurt and that she would be to see him as soon as possible and that she loved him. She said she would hold it down for them while he was on lock down.

After finishing her phone conversation, Carmen gathered some clothes and went to the new apartment she had arranged for them.

Once she got there, she noticed she missed several calls from Poochie, which she really didn't care about. Her mind was so focused on the fact that if it wasn't for the stunt Poochie pulled, Montana and them wouldn't be in the situation they were in.

After getting her things together she called the lawyer again and then headed down the way to get her something to smoke.

She drove around trying to clear her head up. She went home and got in her new tub and smoked, relaxed and thought about what was to come. She thought about if this situation was to ever happen, what she would do and now that it did happen, it wasn't the same situation she had predicted.

*I just hope for the worst and pray for the best,* she thought to herself as she let out a big cloud of smoke. A tear fell from her eyes.

"I want my baby home," she said as a prayer.

---KQP---

Several months had gone past with the incident between Poochie and Mack and the cause of them getting caught up and though Poochie had stolen from him, Mack found himself still having feelings for her. Mack needed her. He had tried at least once a week to get through to her over the phone, only to get refused.

One day he called her phone on a three-way call. When Poochie picked up, Mack hurried up and said, "Poochie I need to talk to you …" Before being hung up on. Poochie wasn't feeling Mack and she really didn't want to hear anything he had to say.

She sat in the living room thinking of a way to get an understanding with Carmen. She really didn't mean for her actions to get Montana and them caught up. Her whole intentions were to fuck Mack over and make a better way for Lil' Shorty, who in her heart she really liked and wanted to build something with.

Poochie wanted to go up to *Ladies First* salon, but she didn't want to create a scene or be confronted with a fight, which she wasn't ready for.

During a conversation she had with Lil' Shorty, she asked Lil' Shorty if he could get Carmen to speak to her.

Things had changed for her during the past four months. She wasn't doing coke anymore. She had successfully completed an outpatient program and was back in school taking up a nursing trade. She was also talking to Lil' Shorty over the phone and she was providing him with everything he needed. Poochie even talked to his lawyer to see if there was anything she could do on his behalf to get him out. The lawyer basically told Poochie that it was a waiting period, because the prosecutor didn't want the lawyer to lower their $500,000 bond to something reasonable.

She wanted to visit him, but by her not ever getting in touch with the detectives, they charged her with drug possession for the crack rocks she got caught with on the Compound and put a warrant out for her arrest.

She was doing everything she could do to make things easier for Lil' Shorty. She was thinking about Lil' Shorty when her phone rang. When she answered, it was Mack calling her. She would usually hang up, but she finally answered.

*"Hello ... hello!"* Mack said. She realized that she answered his call.

"Yeah what's up!" she said.

*"I see you ain't fucking with me huh?"*

"Is this what you keep calling me for?"

*"I been calling you trying to see how you was doing, since I haven't heard nothing from you,"* he tried to say in a nice manner.

"Why you want to know how I'm doing, you wasn't so much worried about me when you was slapping me, nigga!" Poochie said, "why now?"

*"I now realize how much potential you have and I miss you,"* Mack said trying to run his game on her.

"Listen Mack, I'm not even gonna waste your or my time. I fuck with Lil' Shorty, your a fuck nigga for all the shit you did and I'll never talk to your foul ass!"

Mack yelled, *"I took care of you. I showed you the finer things in life and you go and steal my shit and give it to another nigga!"*

"I sure did and I gave it to my real man!" Poochie said laughing and hanging up in his face. She vowed to never accept another call from him again.

"I can't believe this fool, the jokes on you fool," Poochie said grabbing her purse, thinking about the plan she was about to put down.

Mack hung the phone after being hung up on. Mack stood there in a daze. He couldn't believe Poochie was putting it down like that on him. He had been there for her. He had been there for her and her habits, since the first night they met.

"This bitch had the nerve to take my shit and give it to another nigga, I got something for that ass!" Mack said dialing a three-digit number on the phone. When the recording machine picked up he said, "this is Marcus Smith and I'd like to talk to Detective Folley or Prosecutor Debra Baker, I think I have some information that could help them." He hung up and went to his bunk.

Mack had been locked down for four months and his life had flipped upside down. He found out somebody had broken into his apartment and stole all of his furniture, clothes and the rest of the money he had put up. He tried to get at some of the people he knew, but the wrath of Montana had hit him and nobody was looking out for him or doing nothing for him. Mack was angry, worried and wondering about what was to come.

He had called Carmen several months back and she asked him if she was going to help Montana get out. He couldn't believe she had the nerve to ask him some shit like that.

"Fuck Montana!" Mack said punching his bunk, "fuck him he's not nobody!" He started making up his plan to get out of jail.

Two days had gone past, since he left the message on the machine and when the CO called his name, it startled him. They told him that he had an attorney visit.

When he made his way up the stairs to the visiting area, there were two detectives, the prosecutor and his lawyer. He instantly broke into a sweat walking into the room. His lawyer looked at him, not knowing what he was up to.

Detective Folley spoke up, "we got the message you left and you say you got some information for us, but we couldn't talk to you without your lawyer being present. Now that all of us is present, what do you have."

"I think I can help y'all in our drug case," Mack said.

"What makes you want to help now?" Prosecutor Baker asked.

"I feel that it's only right that y'all know the truth, plus I want to be able to help myself from the trouble I'm facing."

"What do you know?" asked the detective.

"I know who drugs is whose and where the drugs come from and I'm willing to help y'all if y'all can help me," Mack said as he squirmed around in his chair.

The detectives and the prosecutor walked out of the room for a few minutes. His lawyer jumped up and said, "why didn't you tell me this was your plan before you hired me?" The lawyer sat back down.

The detectives and the prosecutor walked back in the room with a pen and tablet.

"Write down what you know," they told him. Mack thought for a second, *bitch! See what you made me do!* Then he began writing.

The detective told Marcus that in case Montana was to go to trial he would have to say it in front of a jury which he quickly agreed to.

After doing all he could do, he went back to his block feeling relieved of the pressure, it wasn't a straight shot, but he tried.

---KQP---

Detective Folley headed back to the 3rd district police station after leaving the county. He felt honored that he took Montana Jones and the three other drug dealers off the streets. He wanted their case to go federal, but the US District Attorney wasn't sure of the search warrants or the witness and sent the case back to Cuyahoga County. He just had to get another witness willing to turn states against Montana and with one more witness the deal would be sealed.

He turned to his desk and checked some files on the name of Patrice (Poochie) Day. Not only was she the one with the warrant, she also had called and left a message for him to call her as soon as possible.

He quickly grabbed his phone and dialed the number that was written down. After letting it ring a few times, a female answered.

*"Hello,"* Poochie answered.

"Yes Ms. Day this is Detective Folley from the 3rd district police station."

*"Yes I know who you are."*

"Well what can I do for you, Ms. Day?"

*"Well I think I can help you with some information I have."*

"Concerning what?"

*"A few months ago I got caught up with some drugs and you told me to call you if I found out something about the shootings and drugs that's been happening in Longwood and Outhwaite Estates."*

"You have some valid information about who?"

*"Montana Jones, Michael Jones and Marcus Smith."*

"How can this benefit you, the detective?"

*"Well I want to clear that warrant off of me and get the money from the reward."*

"What do you know?"

*"Well I was with Marcus at my house when he had those drugs and Montana Jones and Michael Jones was there too. Plus, I know who did the shootings on E. 40th Street with the same people as well."*

"Okay Ms. Day, I'll need you to come down here to the precinct and turn yourself in. Once we get your warrant taken care of, you'll be given a statement form to fill out. After doing the statement you will be released.

You're able to have an attorney present if you need one. If this information is not true, you may be charged with perjury and your charge may be picked up by the State of Ohio."

Poochie said, *"okay,"* and hung up the phone.

After the phone conversation with Poochie the detective called the prosecutor and informed her on the new witness and the information she spoke about.

An hour later, Poochie showed up at the 3rd district police station. She got checked and booked in. They brought her out to an empty room beside a table and chair. She sat down as the two detectives and the prosecutor walked in the room sitting a tablet and a pen in front of her.

They told her of her rights before introducing themselves, with the head detective Folley leading the questions.

He asked her, "did you call me or did I call you for this information?"

"I called you to turn myself in," Poochie answered.

"Okay what do you know?" he asked her giving her a choice to either roll or fold. She told the prosecutor about the drugs that was over her apartment with Montana, Michael and Marcus being there. She also told them that Mack told her about the shooting with Dee-Dee's people. She picked the pen up and wrote down what happened.

# Chapter Forty-One

## *Montana*

Montana sat in the County Jail for the past four months. He had high hopes of winning his drug case. The detectives tried to get the case bonded over to the Feds and it was rejected. He knew something was messed up in the case and decided to go to trial.

During the waiting period Montana got the worst shock in the world when his lawyer visited him and told him that Marcus Smith and Patrice Day had turned states and was willing to testify against him.

"What!" Montana said, "who is Patrice Day?" Montana asked. His lawyer let him read the statements.

*Poochie,* Montana said to himself.

"What the fuck!" he said pacing the floor.

"You know that the prosecutor only wants you in this case right, and the way it's looking your gonna be by yourself," the lawyer said.

"What's the deal they're offering me?" Montana asked.

"Well the detectives want to go to trial with the witnesses he has, but the prosecutor said 18 years."

"I can't do 18 years for a plea deal! I might as well go to trial!"

"We got a shot at winning a trial with the deals they're trying to offer," the lawyer said.

"Well go back and see if they will lower the deal or we can get ready for trial," Montana said. He grabbed the statements and walked back to his pod upset.

Later on that day Carmen went and visited Montana. He told her about the statements Mack and Poochie had written against him and Lil' Shorty and the deals that they offered him and Lil' Shorty. He told her that he was taking his case to trial, because they searched the house on an illegal search warrant and the witnesses wasn't reliable.

Carmen told him that she had talked to the lawyer and he was saying they couldn't say who drugs was who's, but with the statement against him there's a bad look that things could go either way. Carmen told Montana about the phone call Lil' Shorty had and he told her that Poochie wanted to talk to her.

"I don't know what she want to talk to me about," Carmen said. Montana told her to talk to Poochie to see what she was talking about. He was starting trial the next week and he wanted to know why she was putting him down.

# Chapter Forty-Two

## Carmen and Poochie

Carmen left the county jail and rushed home. She was already crying every day at the fact that Montana was in jail, but now that Mack and Poochie had written statements against him and Lil' Shorty, that fact alone hurt her more.

She laid back on her couch thinking about what she could do to help them. She picked her phone up and called Kim. Carmen told Kim everything that was going on with Montana. Kim told her that the detectives in Dade County, Miami were looking for the person responsible for Juan's and a bystander's death and the robbery of Chino.

After discussing everything with Kim. Carmen was trying to come up with a plan, but she had to see what Poochie was up to. She looked through her caller ID for Poochie's phone number. She found her number and she realized that Poochie had been calling her for months. She dialed her number and Poochie picked up the phone.

*"Hello,"* Poochie answered.

"May I speak to Poochie," Carmen asked.

*"This is me."*

"Poochie, this Carmen, I need to talk to you."

Poochie began to speak, *"Carmen, I know your probably mad at me and believe me I cherish everything you have showed me and despite how things look, it ain't what you think. I love Lil' Shorty and I'd never do anything to hurt him or his family."*

She was telling her about trying to get with her to tell her about the plan she was putting down to help Lil' Shorty and Montana.

After hearing her out, Carmen told her about what Kim had planned. Poochie jumped on it asking for the detective's number in Dade County.

Carmen half believed her. She told her if she needed anything for her to call her. She hung up the phone and rethought their conversation.

She didn't know for sure and she didn't know if she should trust Poochie. Carmen had to think positive, as she thought of Montana and the news she had for him.

*Trial*
*Friday February 9, 2002*
*Afternoon Session*

After picking the jury that morning, Montana Jones and Michael Jones sat at a table with their lawyers going against the charges they were faced with. The courtroom was packed with friends and family members, reporters and ten white and two black person jury. Along with the head detectives Folley and his partner Thompson. Debra Baker was their prosecutor.

The bailiff came out saying, "all rise you're in the courtroom of the Honorable Judge Joseph Russo, you may be seated."

"This here is case no. CR413675 State of Ohio vs. Montana Jones and Michael Jones," the judge said, explaining the case and introducing everyone to each other before he started the trial.

"Is there anyone with any concerns or objections they want to present?" the judge asked.

*Mr. Paul Manning*

"Yes, I have judge, with regards to the case. I filed a motion to suppress the evidence against my client.

*The Court*

"Motion denied, you may proceed, is there anything else."

*The Court*

"I want to welcome you to Cuyahoga Court of Common Pleas. I am Judge Joseph Russo. I'll be presiding at the proceedings for which you've been summoned in this case. Wednesday morning session February 9, 2002 opening statement on behalf of the State.

*Ms. Baker*

"Thank you, good morning. I'll give you all a briefing on the charges against each of these two individuals. On about July 24, 2001, Montana and Michael Jones did unlawfully and unknowingly obtain, possess or used a schedule II drug in an amount greater than 1000 grams.

"Ladies and gentlemen, what we believe the evidence will show is that on July 24, 2001 Detective Folley, a member of the Cleveland Police Department Vice Unit had in his possession a search warrant for a location in the City of Cleveland. That location being 469 Woodland Avenue. There are actually two buildings, he can see right down the alley across Woodland Avenue from where he was sitting in the back as he set up surveillance. He had two individuals going into the premises. Those individuals were Montana Jones and Marcus Smith, at some point, as they're watching, they seen the male identified, later as Israel Witherman run toward the apartment. At this point CMHA officers jumped out of their car to stop Mr. Witherman who runs into the unit and the detectives followed him in."

"Detective Ramsey, who is the second man, looked into the kitchen and you can see people in the kitchen. Ramsey went into the kitchen where he sees their people, Montana Jones, Michael Jones and Marcus Smith. If you see me hesitating, it's because I don't want to misname who I'm talking about."

"Detective Ramsey sees Montana Jones standing by the kitchen, excuse me, see him by the kitchen sink, Marcus Smith by the window and Michael Jones in the doorway. He ordered them all to the floor. Michael Jones and Marcus Smith went down to the floor. Mr. Montana Jones is a little hesitant, but the detective convinces him to also hit the floor. They were detained patted down and cuffed."

"Now what the detective found in the premises we believe the evidence will show is this on the kitchen counter, several packages wrapped containing powder, that later tested positive to be cocaine. We believe that Mr. Witherman and Marcus Smith will offer testimony that they were running drugs for Montana Jones."

Montana's lawyer spoke against the prosecutor and said, "ladies and gentlemen. I anticipate once you've heard all of the facts, that you're going to find that Montana Jones is not guilty of the crimes he's charged with, thank you."

Opening Statements on Behalf of Defendant Michael Jones
*Mr. Dennis*

"The evidence is going to show that Mr. Smith who is looking at 22 years, realized that he is in a wringer. He then decides he's going to cut a deal. What does he do, he blames it on Michael Jones. The evidence is going to show; he'll get some lesser sentence when he testifies."

*The Court*

"State you may call your next witness."

*Mr. Dennis*

"No your honor."

*The Court*

"State you may call your next witness."

*Ms. Baker*

"The State calls Detective Ramsey to the stand."

*Detective Ramsey*

After telling his background as a detective, he told how he seen a big bag of cocaine and Montana Jones was the closest one to it, He also said how he seen Israel Witherman and Michael Jones going to the apartment, the day they were arrested.

Ms. Baker called her police witnesses to the stand, then she called Israel Witherman who testified to the statement that he wrote and the deal he was looking forward to and once the defense cross examines him, the State called Patrice Day to the stand.

*Ms. Baker*

Q. "Ms. Day do you know Montana Jones and Michael Jones?"

A. "Yes."

Q. "How do you know them?"

A. "They came over my house with Marcus Smith, my ex-boyfriend."

Q. "Was you promised anything for your testimony?"

A. "No, I came on my own to tell the truth."

Q. "Could you tell the jury what you seen at the apartment?"

A. I seen Marcus Smith walking in carrying a large bag of cocaine underneath his jacket."

Q. "Did you see Montana Jones and Michael with any drugs?"

A. "No, me and Marcus Smith went and got them from Miami, Florida."

"Your honor may I approach the bench?" Ms. Baker asked.

*The Court*

"You may. Jury, take a 15-minute break," Judge Russo instructed the them.

*Ms. Baker*

"Your honor, Ms. Day just deliberately perjured herself and may have cost me this case."

*The Court*

"Ms. Day you have perjured yourself and you're in contempt of court." The bailiff cuffed her and took her to the back. The jury came back after Poochie was arrested for contempt of court.

*The Court*

"The State may call its next witness."

*Ms. Baker*

"The State call Marcus Smith to the stand."

Q. "Mr. Smith did you get promised anything for your testimony?"

A. "No, I'm hoping to get help."

Q. "How do you know Montana Jones and Michael Jones?"

A. "I grew up with them in he projects of Cleveland."

Q. "Did you write a statement?"

A. "Yes."

Q. "Is it true? Could you read it?"

A. "Yes!" He started reading the statement.

Q. "Was you at 469 Woodland Avenue during the arrest?"

A. "Yes, I was there. I got arrested too."

Q. "What happened?"

A. "Montana Jones had a large bag of drugs and Michael Jones was helping him prepare it, as myself and Israel tested its quality. Israel ran in the apartment with the police chasing him. They found Montana Jones' drugs and charged all of us."

*Ms. Baker*

"Nothing further your honor."

*The Court*

"Cross Examination of Marcus Smith."


*Paul Manning*

Q. "You were arrested too right?"

A. "Right."

Q. "How much time are you facing if you don't testify?"

A. "I don't know; I think 20 years."

Q. "Twenty years you say?"

A. "Yes."

Q. "So is the time making you turn and push the weight on them?"

A. "No, I want them to get what they got coming to them."

*Paul Manning*

"Nothing further your honor."

<u>*Mr. Dennis*</u>

Q. "You say you were with them?"

    A. "Yes."

Q. "You called the detective or prosecutor for a deal?"

A. "Yes."

Q. "Did you tell the truth then or now?"

A. "Now, I got to tell the truth."

Q. "How much do you want to be home?"

A. "A whole lot."

Q. "More than having a lot of money."

A. "Yes."

"Nothing further your honor."

Montana sat at the trial table across from Detective Folley and Prosecutor Baker. A few times he looked in Folley's direction and Folley would look at him with a little smirk on his face, because the witnesses were shooting heavy statements against him and it wasn't looking good for him.

Lil' Shorty sat there with tears in his eyes. Hadn't he let Montana change his mind about giving Mack those drugs back, they might not be sitting in court.

Mack got up on the stand and said it was them that had the drugs, when in reality he knew it was his drugs. Then the fiend ass dude Witherman gets on the stand saying what part he played. Like he doesn't know how the game goes.

Lil' Shorty and Montana didn't take the stand in their own defense, because of their prior records. Poochie had said a lot in her testimony. They thought she was with the State considering she had wrote a statement saying she knew them and that they were at her apartment with the drugs. Come to find out she made an opening for them.

Poochie had really pissed the prosecutor and detective off. They threw her in jail before the jury were able to hear her whole testimony.

She told Lil' Shorty she had another one of her plans to help them better their future. Her getting on the stand and flipping the script on them had him starting to believe her when she said she had something else up her sleeve.

They sat there in front of the jury as the Judge sent them out to deliberate. They looked back at all of their family and friends. Sue, Moe and Momma Lucy sat next to Carmen. They were smiling giving them the thumbs up.

Lil' Shorty and Montana had a good chance at winning their case. They were sent back to their cells, while the jury deliberated. That turned into a four-day wait.

When the bailiff came to get them, there were so many thoughts going through their minds. Montana sat there waiting for the Judge and jury to seal his fate.

Thursday Afternoon Session, February 13, 2002

Verdict

*The Court*

"We're back on the record for trial case no. CR513075. State of Ohio Vs Michael Jones and Montana Jones."

*The Court*

"Ladies and Gentlemen of the jury have you elected a foreperson?"

*Mr. Wise*

"Yes we have."

*The Court*

"Has the jury reached a verdict?"

*Mr. Wise*

"Yes we have."

*The Court*

"If you could give the verdict to Angela, my staff attorney. Will defendant, Michael Jones, please stand. We the jury in this case being duly impaneled and sworn, this is on Count 1 Possession of Drugs, do find the defendant, Michael Jones not guilty of possession of drugs as charged in Count 1 of the indictment. Count 2, we the jury in this case being duly impaneled and sworn, do find the defendant Michael Jones, not guilty of possession of drugs, to wit cocaine a schedule II drug, as charged in count 2 of the indictment.

Lil' Shorty jumped up and said, "yeah, I told you I was coming home!" The judge banged his gavel to control the people.

*The Court*

"We the jury in this case being duly impaneled and sworn, do find the defendant, Montana Jones, not guilty of possession of drugs to wit, cocaine schedule II drug as charged in Count 1 of the indictment."

"Further finding we the jury in this case find that the defendant Montana Jones is not guilty of possession of drugs and further find that the amount of the controlled substance in Count 2 to wit, cocaine a scheduled II drug was in the amount greater than 1000 grams with regard to defendant Montana Jones."

"Is this the verdict of all 12 of the jurors?" Judge Russo asked.

"Yes."

Everybody in the courtroom jumped up and cheered. Montana and Lil' Shorty hugged, while Sue, Moe, Ms. Lucy and Carmen rushed them with tears of joy in their eyes. They all hugged their lawyers.

Detective Folley looked angry screaming out loud, "they're guilty! They're guilty! They got caught red handed with drugs! They're guilty!"

He kept saying with a furious red face, "I'll get you! I'll get you!"

Montana smiled at him and said, "do your job." He walked out the courtroom with the biggest smile on his face.

Come to find out, Poochie made a deal for herself with the prosecutor to testify against Mack for the attempted murder and felonious assault against Dee-Dee.

Kim and Chino came to testify against Mack for the murder of Juan and the robbery of Chino. Mack took a plea deal of 48 years opposed to the death penalty.

Montana and Lil' Shorty went home to everything intact. Carmen had held shit down, telling Montana he came up. Montana told her that he came up when he met her.

Montana's Come Up!

# About the Author

I'm Marvin Lamont Loper (MTG). I'm 44 years old and I was born and raised in the inner city of Cleveland, in the projects where growing up was a book in itself. Learning and seeing life throughout the struggles showed me enough to sit down and tell a story of how it all went down.

To all the big homies that walked before me and showed me how to put it down, thanks because it would've been harder. It was a gift and a curse though. I've learned from a curse now my gift is coming forth. I've wrote my book Montana's Come Up and I'm in the process of finishing my second book, Welcome to the Streets. I look to open eyes, because throughout life, we then seen it all in the streets.

MTG – Montana the Great

Made in the
USA
Monee, IL